Kendall McCormick's answering machine: Hi, it's Kendall. I'm getting married today! I'll be gone on my honeymoon, but if you want to sign up for swim lessons, or just say hello, please leave your name and number after the beep. Sorry I missed you!

Message #1: Uh, Kendall? This is Darren. Listen, I wanted to catch you before you left for the church. I won't be able to make it to our wedding. Something's come up. You can handle this. Right? I'm really sorry. I'll call you when I get back in town. And—Kendall? If you happen to hear from my brother, Rafe—well, I'd advise you to avoid him. Okay?

Message #2: Kendall McCormick? It's Rafe Tennyson, Darren's brother. I'm coming over to see you. We need to talk.

Message #3: Kendall? It's Kim. Where are you? Everyone's going nuts looking for you. Greg says he saw you riding off with a man in a sports car. Should we call the police?

Reluctant Grooms
1. Lazarus Rising
   Anne Stuart
2. A Million Reasons Why
   Ruth Jean Dale
3. Designs on Love
   Gina Wilkins
4. The Nesting Instinct
   Elizabeth August
5. Best Man for the Job
   Dixie Browning
6. Not *His* Wedding!
   Suzanne Simms

Western Weddings
7. The Bridal Price
   Barbara Boswell
8. McCade's Woman
   Rita Rainville
9. Cactus Rose
   Stella Bagwell
10. The Cowboy and the Chauffeur
    Elizabeth August
11. Marriage-Go-Round
    Katherine Ransom
12. September Morning
    Diana Palmer

Instant Families
13. Circumstantial Evidence
    Annette Broadrick
14. Bundle of Joy
    Barbara Bretton
15. McConnell's Bride
    Naomi Horton
16. A Practical Marriage
    Dallas Schulze
17. Love Counts
    Karen Percy
18. Angel and the Saint
    Emilie Richards

Marriage, Inc.
19. Father of the Bride
    Cathy Gillen Thacker
20. Wedding of the Year
    Elda Minger
21. Wedding Eve
    Betsy Johnson
22. Taking a Chance on Love
    Gina Wilkins
23. This Day Forward
    Elizabeth Morris
24. The Perfect Wedding
    Arlene James

Make-Believe Matrimony
25. The Marriage Project
    Lynn Patrick
26. It Happened One Night
    Marie Ferrarella
27. Married?!
    Annette Broadrick
28. In the Line of Duty
    Doreen Roberts
29. Outback Nights
    Emilie Richards
30. Love for Hire
    Jasmine Cresswell

Wanted: Spouse
31. Annie in the Morning
    Curtiss Ann Matlock
32. Mail-Order Mate
    Louella Nelson
33. A Business Arrangement
    Kate Denton
34. Mail Order Man
    Roseanne Williams
35. Silent Sam's Salvation
    Myrna Temte
36. Marry Sunshine
    Anne McAllister

Runaway Brides
37. Runaway Bride
    Karen Leabo
38. Easy Lovin'
    Candace Schuler
39. Madeline's Song
    Stella Bagwell
40. Temporary Temptress
    Christine Rimmer
41. Almost a Bride
    Raye Morgan
42. Strangers No More
    Naomi Horton

Solution: Wedding
43. To Choose a Wife
    Phyllis Halldorson
44. A Most Convenient Marriage
    Suzanne Carey
45. First Comes Marriage
    Debbie Macomber
46. Make-believe Marriage
    Carole Buck
47. Once Upon a Time
    Lucy Gordon
48. Taking Savanah
    Pepper Adams

Please address questions and book requests to: Silhouette Reader Service
U.S.: 3010 Walden Ave., P.O. Box 1325, Buffalo, NY 14269
Canadian: P.O. Box 609, Fort Erie, Ont. L2A 5X3

Runaway Brides

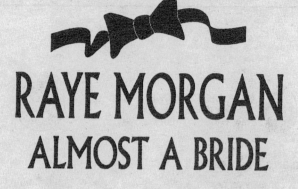

RAYE MORGAN
ALMOST A BRIDE

Published by Silhouette Books
America's Publisher of Contemporary Romance

SILHOUETTE BOOKS
300 East 42nd St.,
New York, N.Y. 10017

ISBN 0-373-30141-3

ALMOST A BRIDE

Copyright © 1992 by Helen Conrad

Celebrity Wedding Certificates published by permission of
Donald Ray Pounders from *Celebrity Wedding Ceremonies*.

Printed in U.S.A.

A Letter from the Author

Dear Reader,

Love at first sight…soul mates…a perfect match…true love…happily ever after—are these concepts just a lot of fairy-tale myths to weave stories around?

You hear that a lot, especially from the current popular media. It's a cynical age we live in. That's why romances are so special to a lot of us. I still believe in all those old clichés—and so do you, or you wouldn't be reading this book!

The wedding is the ultimate expression of romance. The heroine who gets close and then seems to lose it all is one of the most tragic figures we write about. But what if her sorrow and disappointment are for the best? What if they only set up a better relationship with another man—and set the stage for a much better wedding?

That's what happens in *Almost a Bride*. Darren doesn't show and Kendall runs off in her wedding dress, not realizing that the man she hitches a ride with is Darren's brother, Rafe, who is under the impression that she is a schemer. I hope you enjoy the tug-of-war between Rafe and Kendall. They were a fun couple to write about and I was thrilled to find they would be included in the HERE COME THE GROOMS series. Thanks!

Raye Morgan

One

He wasn't coming.

Kendall McCormick pulled at the long, lace sleeves of her wedding gown and glanced nervously out the view hole at the congregation again. This was too much. What was she supposed to do, go before them all and make the announcement? "Sorry folks, but Darren has decided he doesn't want to marry me after all. You can all go home. The dream is over."

Her stomach flip-flopped and she began to pace again.

"Kendall!" The door to the bride's room opened and Kim peered around it, eyes full of panic. "Where could he be? The organist has another service across town and she can't wait much longer...."

Kendall turned and tried to smile. "I don't think he's coming," she said clearly, her words firm, her tone even. "I've been stood up at the altar." It was the first time she had actually said it out loud.

"Oh, my God, no!" Kim wailed, hands to her pretty face. "I don't believe it. He's just…late. A flat tire, maybe…" Her voice trailed off. The eternal optimist, even she didn't buy it any longer. "I'll go wait downstairs," she said, her voice teary. "If I see him, I'll run right up." She hesitated. "You're all right, aren't you? You're—you're not going to cry or anything?"

Kendall stood very still, her dark eyes clear and steady. "No, of course not."

"Oh…" Kim wrung her hands tragically. Her plump cheeks were bright red. "I just know he's coming. Don't you worry, honey. He'll be here soon."

"Sure."

Sure. Right. As if.

There was no way Darren was coming now. It was just too darn late.

Kendall turned as the door closed again and Kim's high-heel shoes clattered on the stairs. She looked into the long, cold mirror, studied the long, satin gown with its delicate covering of alençon lace, the pearl-studded bodice of crushed velvet with its off-the-shoulders neckline, the graceful chapel train. Her chocolate-colored hair was piled high like an old-fashioned Gibson girl's. She looked just like the brides in all the magazines.

She was ready. Everything was perfect. What had gone wrong?

Slowly, her gaze panned from her satin shoes up past the lace, the satin sash, the tight bodice, the pearls, the filmy veil—and then she met her own eyes in the reflection, and her white teeth flashed a vivid grin.

"Thank God," she said loud and clear. "I'm out of here."

Turning so fast that her skirt flew out in an arc, she grabbed a pad of paper and a pen, jotting down a quick note. "Sorry Mom," it said, "to leave you to deal with this mess. Forgive me, but I have to get away and be alone for a while. I'll call."

She set the pad where it couldn't be missed and turned. Gathering her skirts in her arms, she made it to the back steps and bolted like a horse let out into spring pasture, past the doors to the sanctuary, past the preacher's office, down the steps and into the sunlight. She had no idea where she was going or how she would get there. She only knew she needed to get out, needed to badly.

Out among the cars in the parking lot, she faltered. She had come in a limousine. How was she going to get where she wanted to go without a car?

"Hello," said a deep, resonant voice from close beside her. "It's Kendall, isn't it? The bride?"

She looked down. The man at the wheel of the late-model sports-car convertible was tall and lean and rangy, like a cowboy in a business suit. He must have been a friend of Darren's; she'd never seen him before. "I was almost the bride," she said with a far-away look in her eyes. "Now I'm a runaway."

The man looked startled, dark eyebrows drawing together. "Oh?"

She glanced down at him again. He was a hand-some man, in a hard, dark way, with good solid shoulders, the kind just made for crying on. Too bad he wasn't a friend of hers. She could use that kind of friend right now.

"If you've come for the wedding," she told him, "you might as well turn around and go home. There's not going to be one."

"No?"

"No." She looked toward the horizon, toward where the sun was heading for the ocean, drawing her. That was where she wanted to go, too.

"I see you're leaving yourself."

"Yes." Looking down at him, she smiled. When opportunity presented itself, who was she to turn it away? "Which direction are you headed? I could use a ride."

The blue eyes, so striking against his tan skin, seemed to darken to a steely gray. "Hop in," he said without a pause. "I'll take you anywhere you want to go."

She hesitated. She didn't know him, but he was invited to the wedding, so somebody obviously did. Besides, after what she'd gone through, she was in no mood to be fastidious. She just wanted to get out of here, fast.

"Thanks," she said, and he leaned across to open the passenger's door for her. She slipped into the plush leather seat, cramming her dress in around her, heedless of wrinkles now, and they were off, the wind lashing at her veil.

"Do you have a destination in mind?" he asked above the roar of the British engine.

She shook her head, then looked toward where the basin opened up to the sea. He nodded, understanding without being told, and turned onto the main street. She sighed, leaning back in the seat, letting the wind slap around her as though it might cleanse her of all trouble. This was going to be great.

"Leave the past behind," she whispered to herself, too low for him to hear. "Away we go."

Kendall didn't speak as they traveled down Colorado Boulevard, and neither did her driver. As he made the left turn onto Arroyo Parkway, he managed to get a good look at her. And that was lucky, because he needed another look. She wasn't at all what he'd expected.

But then, what exactly had he expected?

He'd never heard of Kendall before the previous evening when he'd received a telephone call from Darren.

"Hey, Rafe, your one and only brother is getting married tomorrow. Want to come over and join in the wake?"

He and Darren were not close. The only time Rafe ever heard from his younger sibling was when he was in need of something—usually money. So he had assumed right from the start that this was a cry for help.

The bachelor party had been loud, smoky and very crowded. Darren had always maintained a wide selection of friends. By the time Rafe arrived, the man of the hour was already two sheets to the wind, unable to do much more than murmur, "She's a wonderful girl, you're going to love her," and grin idiotically as he reached for another bourbon on the rocks.

Rafe turned to Darren's closest friends for a bit of background. "What's she like?" he quizzed Binko, Darren's old fraternity brother.

Binko squinted hard, revving up his meager brain-power, and answered, "Gee, Rafe, I'm not sure if she's the blonde with the great tan or the Hawaiian girl with the navel you could dive into..."

Rafe continued to hunt around for someone who had actual firsthand acquaintanceship. Finally, after working the room for half an hour, he found Dorchester, who worked with Darren at the Border Cantina and claimed to have met the bride-to-be.

"Kendall McCormick is her name. And she's gorgeous, of course. All Darren's women are gorgeous." He shook his head with the disgust of someone who wasn't quite as lucky himself.

"What's she like?" Rafe asked shortly.

"What's she like?" Dorchester grunted, rolling his eyes. "I'll tell you what she's like. Hair as thick and rich as the frosting on a devil's food cake and longer than you could believe anyone could grow it. Legs that stretch from here until tomorrow...."

"But what is she *like?*" Rafe interjected impatiently.

Dorchester was lost in a rhapsody of memory, his eyes glazed. "You should see her, the way she walks. Hey, she's got a body that would make a whole block of construction workers lie down and beg for mercy. She's got this way of tossing her hair back over her shoulder..."

Rafe gave up at that point. Kendall McCormick sounded like a carbon copy of every other woman Darren had dated since puberty. And he had dated a lot. What Rafe wanted to know was what this woman had that made her different from the rest. Why was Darren marrying *her?*

He finished his drink, gave appreciative attention to the stripper, then watched in apprehension as his brother took to singing old Irish songs in a voice that could grind diamonds. Rafe had maintained for years that the act of matrimonial bondage was one of the most degrading things a man could do to himself, and from the looks of it, his brother was going to bear out his judgment.

Finally Rafe shrugged and turned for the door. There didn't seem much point in staying. If Darren was intent upon committing this folly, there wasn't much Rafe could do to stop him. If only he could shake the queasy feeling that Darren wasn't exactly thrilled with the prospect himself.

He'd almost made a clean getaway when a voice from behind stopped him cold.

"Where do you think you're going? Aren't you going to help him? You can't just leave him like this. He's your brother, for God's sake."

Rafe turned to find Sam, who'd been a buddy of Darren's since elementary school, almost in tears, his freckled face contorted with alcohol-aided anguish.

"Get a grip, Sam," Rafe snapped. "Darren's a full-grown man. He can take care of himself and make his own decisions."

"Not this time, Rafe." Sam took up a stranglehold on Rafe's lapels. "The woman's cast a spell over him. She's tricked him. She's cornered him. You can't leave him to twist slowly in the wind. You've gotta help."

"Help? How can I help?"

"You're the cause of all this anguish. And you can do something the rest of us can't."

Rafe had no idea what Sam was talking about, and he was pretty sure he didn't really want to know. He continued to edge toward the door. "What can I possibly do?"

"You can talk him out of it, that's what." Sam slapped an arm around Rafe's shoulders. "Come on back in and I'll tell you the whole story."

Reluctantly, Rafe had turned back. He'd known he was going to regret it. He'd also known he wouldn't get a lot of sleep that night. But he hadn't realized he would end up with the would-be bride in his car, racing toward the ocean.

Now he glanced at her once again. No, she didn't fit his preconception at all. He'd expected someone a little bold, a little brassy and very, very upset. Instead . . .

She was stretched out in the seat beside him like a woman at ease with her body. In fact, she looked pretty much at ease with life in general. What was going on here? She'd just been left standing at the altar. Common sense called for a good gush of anger. Perhaps a whimper. At the very least, a bitter smile.

But when he looked her way, she turned and grinned, and said, "Hey, this is really fun."

He turned back to his driving with a frown. Something was very wrong with this picture.

Kendall reached up to brace her veil on her head as they swept around a steep curve and headed into Los Angeles. Closing her eyes, she let her head fall back and welcome the stinging wind. It was going to be all right. It was, after all, for the best.

Wasn't it?

There was a tiny catch in her breathing as her heart skipped a beat, but she pushed the doubt away again. Darren had only done what she should have done herself. This match had not been made in heaven, and that had been apparent for a long time. She should have known from the start. She wasn't going to mourn for something that had never been real. At least she was going to try very hard not to. There was no point to it.

Still, she was going to be a little crazy for a while. She could sense that. She was going to need comfort—not an arm-around-the-shoulders-and-a-pat-on-the-back sort of comfort—more like someone to go a little crazy with her. Could this nice man driving her to the beach be the one?

She sneaked a glance at him just at the same moment he turned to say something.

"Marina del Rey okay?"

"Yes. That would be perfect."

He nodded, his attention back on his driving. She continued to study him for a moment, really seeing him for the first time and feeling just a trace of unease.

He was hard and long and competent looking, a little rough and ready for the nice dark business suit he wore. The white shirt was open at the throat, revealing more dark skin and a hint of crisp, black, curling hair. No wedding ring. The expensive gold watch he wore was slim and elegant on his wrist.

His face was grooved, whether from smiles or snarls, it was hard to tell. He looked cool, smart and dangerous to deal with. The opposite of Darren, with his sunny surfer-boy appeal and ready laughter. This was a man who would never leave a woman at the altar. This was a man who would never propose unless he really meant it. But she had a feeling that this was also a man who would have a hard time taking no for an answer.

Nice profile. Hard. Strong. Unforgiving.

She shivered and looked away.

Forgiveness. That was a concept she was going to have to wrestle with herself, wasn't she?

For just a moment she had the sinking sensation usually associated with major drops on a roller coaster. Terra firma was slipping away at an awkward angle. Everything had changed. There was a big, black hole where her future used to be.

Oh, Darren, Darren, how could you do this to me?

She closed her eyes and held her breath, pushing regret away. She didn't want to deal with it now. She wasn't ready for it yet.

The air was cooler. They were getting closer to the beach. Her driver took a handy off ramp, and the little car slid into a parking lot and came to a stop just a few yards away from the sand.

"Wonderful." Kendall got out of the car and looked toward the ocean shimmering in the sunlight. She wasn't sure why she needed to be here, but she did. Laughing softly, she kicked off her satin shoes and let her feet sink into the sand, then started briskly toward the water's edge, scooping her billowing skirt up around her knees.

Rafe followed more slowly, watching her, stopping to pick up her shoes and shoving them into the pockets of his suit coat. He glanced quickly up and down the beach. It was spring and the weather was still too cool to crowd the beaches, but there were quite a few people about, some with children, some playing volleyball or tossing a Frisbee along the crusty sand. He almost smiled, wondering what these beach goers were going to make of a bride in her formal gown scampering among them.

Kendall didn't notice the others on the beach. Her attention was focused on the water. The ocean looked lovely, blue and clean and inviting. It reminded her of the beach trips of her childhood, when she would lose herself for hours in the cold water, playing make-believe princess of some underwater kingdom. Some of the happiest times of her life...

There was a lump in her throat. The salty breeze touched her face. A sea gull cried. She began to run. She heard the man coming up behind her, but she didn't turn, and when he grabbed her, sweeping her up into his arms, she gasped in surprise. "Put me down! What do you think you're doing?"

He wasn't about to let go, despite the huge gown snapping and twisting about them both. He glared at her, his arms tightening his hold around her as though afraid she might slip away. "What are *you* doing? That's the question."

She blinked, still not getting it, stiff and awkward in his arms, just a bit wary of him and his dangerous face. "I was just going down to the ocean." Realization dawned and she gave him an incredulous look.

"Did you think you were saving me from the watery depths?" She grinned suddenly, leaning back to get a good look at him. "Very gallant of you, I'm sure, but..." She struggled a bit, trying to squirm her way out of his hold on her. "You can put me down now. The crisis is over."

He didn't give any sign of relenting, his face as hard and strong as his grip on her. "You're not planning to go into the water like this, are you?" he demanded. "I'm not going to let you go until I get some assurance."

"Oh, for Pete's sake." She looked at him again, annoyance tempered by amusement. He was obviously quite serious. He really thought she might be suicidal. It didn't look as though he was going to be the one to go crazy with after all. "Okay. Hand on my heart. I swear I will not cast myself into the murky deep. Okay?"

Rafe searched her dark eyes for a moment. She was firm and slim and athletic, but the wedding gown accentuated her curves, heightening his sense of gender identification. He didn't remember feeling this protective toward a woman in a long time. But then, he hadn't had this much reason before. Still, maybe he was going overboard. Reluctantly, he let her slide down until her feet hit the ground.

She tossed back her veil and grinned at him impudently as she found her footing. "Awfully anxious to play hero, aren't you? Listen, next time I need saving, I'll definitely let you know."

"You don't need a hero, Kendall," he said crisply. "You need a caretaker. At least for the short run."

But Kendall hardly heard him. He'd called her by her name. Of course, he would know it. He'd been coming to her wedding. But she still didn't know his.

"We've never met before, have we?" she asked him, searching his face.

"No." Rafe hesitated, her swift change of subject catching him off guard. He should tell her who he was. The time was right. But for some reason, he didn't want to quite yet. "My name is Rafe," he said shortly, avoiding the last name, which would give away the fact that he was Darren's brother.

"A friend of Darren's," Kendall supplied, nodding, thinking all the while that he was so different from other friends of her ex-fiancé's she had met— older, calmer, more intelligent. Let's face it, she thought, Darren's friends had mostly been scatterbrained playboys with very little to offer other than fun and games. That should have been a sign. How long had she allowed herself to live in this dreamworld, ignoring things like that, pretending Darren really was the one for her? What an idiot. Maybe she really should throw herself into the surf after all.

"Well, here's a clue, Rafe. I'm not the suicidal type. I'm more likely to go for revenge." She flashed him a quick grin meant to hide all her insecurities, even from herself. "So don't try to fling yourself onto every grenade you see before us. None of them are set to go off."

He frowned, his blue eyes charged with something that just might have been skepticism. "Well, think of what a picture you made—a woman in a wedding gown running toward the waves. When you stop and realize that that woman has just been..." His voice faded away and he looked uncomfortable.

She turned slowly and looked at him, only the hint of a smile at the edges of her mouth and eyes. "Jilted?" she supplied helpfully.

He shrugged. That was the word, wasn't it? There was no use pretending any differently.

She stared into his eyes, emotions she hardly recognized churning inside her. What was she feeling? Rage? Fear? Amusement? She hardly knew. "Anyway," she said shortly, "I'm a very good swimmer. If I'd made it out there into the waves, I doubt you could have caught me."

Her eyes flashed, and Rafe had no doubt that she was probably right. He made no reply and she turned and began to walk along the lacy edge of the water, just out of reach of the surf.

Rafe came along behind her, wondering why he felt this overwhelming sense of responsibility toward this woman. After all, she really was a grown adult. She'd made a play for Darren and it hadn't panned out. It was her problem, not his. She'd wanted to go to the beach, and he'd brought her there. Now it was surely time for him to climb back into his car and get out of her life. But something was holding him there.

They trudged along the sand, and he watched her fight the wind for her clothes. "Wouldn't you like to take off that veil, at least?" he asked her at last.

She turned as though surprised to see that he was still with her. "Why? Are you embarrassed to be seen with me?"

"Embarrassed?" He gave her a mock look of astonishment. "Why should I be embarrassed? I'm not the only one everyone's staring at."

Looking around quickly, she noticed he was right. They were something of a center of interest. People were craning toward them, lifting sunglasses to get a better look.

She giggled, twirling to give them a show. "The bride at the beach. Don't you think that's a fun concept? I ought to call the papers. They're always looking for a new beach angle." Stopping in midtwirl, she looked up at him and turned her mouth down sadly. "I guess there's no such thing as the groom at the beach, is there?" she commented. "At least not in my case."

Rafe saw it then for a split second. In a quick flash, a piece of her heartache was revealed in her eyes. He felt his throat contract as it hit him. That was what he had been waiting for, some sign that she was reacting, some evidence that what had happened had sunk in and she was going to be able to deal with it.

She stood there with the raging surf behind her; wisps of her hair scattering across her face, teasing her long eyelashes, dragging across her moist lips; her lacy white veil lashing out behind her. He felt an urge to take her into the protection of his arms again, to hold her against the pain that was surely to come.

"You make a beautiful bride," he heard himself saying.

"You think so?" Her face brightened at the compliment, making him want to think of other nice things to say to her. "You know, I should have had pictures taken before I left. The photographer was there, raring to go. And I know I'll never, *ever* do this again."

"Do what again? Be a bride? Sure you will. You're young, beautiful, you've got your whole life ahead of you."

She laughed softly. He seemed so sincere. "You're awfully nice," she said, pushing the hair back out of her face.

His eyes darkened with a smoky look, meant as a barrier. "No, Kendall," he said huskily, his face hardening along with his tone. "I'm not all that nice."

She stared at him. For some reason, that put her back up. "Oh, I see. It's just pity, is it?" she snapped. Whirling, she began her rush along the shoreline again.

Rafe came along beside her, wincing as sand filled his Italian-leather shoes.

She glanced back, her mouth set. "So how do you know that I was the one left standing at the altar?" she went on accusingly, her hand on her veil. "How do you know I didn't leave Darren wandering the halls, wondering where I'd gone?"

The answer came to her without his having to say a word. Shocked, she spun to a stop and glared at him. "You know him really well, don't you? In fact, you knew there was going to be no wedding when you arrived. Didn't you?"

He didn't bother to try to deny it. There was hardly any point now.

Her hands went to her hips and she took a defensive stance in the sand. "So, tell me, what were his reasons?" she demanded, red spots coloring her cheeks, her dark eyes full of accusation. "No. Let me guess." She pretended to think, head to the side. "Let's see, hmm, he needed to wash his hair? His Porsche was in the shop?"

Her sarcasm was doing very little to mask the pain, but he was glad to see it coming out. She needed to vent.

"No, that's hardly fair, is it?" she went on. "Surely it was something more important. His therapist told him he needed time to center on himself and a wedding would ruin his focus? Or he heard about a rally to protect endangered musk worms and he couldn't miss it. What a guy. A real friend of the earth, you know what I mean?"

"Kendall . . ." Rafe reached toward her, but she stepped back.

"Oh, no, I get it. His astrologer told him the stars weren't right. Jupiter was on a collision course with Mars, and he would be hit by the fallout if he didn't get out of town. Am I getting warmer?"

His hands closed on her shoulders, holding her still. He wanted to pull her to his chest, but he sensed instinctively that she wouldn't allow that. Instead, he threw up a bit of truth for her to chew on. "If this is what you think of him," he said quietly, "why were you planning to marry him?"

She stared at him, her eyes wide and vulnerable. "That is a very good question." He really had her there, and she was ashamed to admit it. Her chin rose defensively. "Like they say, love is blind."

"I see. And being left at the altar suddenly restores twenty-twenty vision?"

Her head jerked back as though he'd slapped her. Her dark eyes mirrored the sting of his words. "Hey, you don't give any slack, do you?" she said softly. Her dark eyes glared at him, then she broke away and began her headlong assault on the shore again.

He came along more reluctantly this time. He'd gotten a reaction, but it wasn't enough. He wanted her to cry. From what he knew of women, that was exactly what she needed.

But when you came right down to it, he wasn't the one who should make her cry or comfort her. What the hell was he doing here, anyway? If he'd thought he would end up like this, he would never have gone racing out to the chapel to tell her Darren wasn't coming. It wasn't as if Darren had asked him to do it.

No one had asked him to do it. He'd sat up all night with his brother and the few of his friends who had lingered into the dawn and listened to Darren cry and moan and feel sorry for himself, until Rafe had finally turned to Sam and asked, "Why do you think he's marrying her?"

"Are you kidding?" Sam retorted. "It's the age-old trick they all play." He made a face that was hard to misinterpret.

Rafe frowned. "You mean . . . she's pregnant?"

Sam shrugged grandly. "How else is any chick going to tie down our roving playboy?"

Rafe turned to stare at his brother, miserable wretch that he had become during the long, plaintive night. "At his age, you would think he would be more careful."

"Darren?" Sam said, misbelieving.

Their eyes met, and Rafe shook his head. "You're right. Being careful has never been one of Darren's virtues. And I suppose it never will."

"So . . . are you going to tell him?"

Rafe knew what he was getting at, but he didn't want to admit it. "Tell him what?"

"That he doesn't have to marry her. That there are other ways to deal with this sort of thing." Sam leaned closer and narrowed his eyes. "That his big brother won't despise him if he backs out."

Rafe frowned again. "He knows that already."

"No." Sam shook his head emphatically. "No, he doesn't know that. All he's been talking about all week is how proud you were going to be of him once he settled down, how you were going to see there was something in him yet." Sam sighed heavily. "You've gotta tell him, Rafe. You've gotta give him permission to back out of this."

Permission to back out. Permission to jilt the girl. It had seemed a simple thing to do. But that was before Rafe had met the woman involved.

Two

Kendall wasn't going to cry, no matter what Rafe might think. She was far from allowing her emotions to do that to her. This wasn't fun, she had to admit. It stung a little. But it was all for the best. She just had to get used to this empty feeling, that was all. Then everything would be fine.

She tripped on a tangle of shiny brown kelp and Rafe reached out to steady her with a hand on her arm. She pulled away from his touch. She didn't need help. She could stand on her own, damn it.

When the tears stung her eyes, they surprised her and she shook them away quickly. But she had to face facts. Who exactly did she think she was kidding? This hurt like hell. The man she had been planning to marry had rejected her. He'd stepped back, taken a second look, shook his head and said, "No, thank you. I think I'll pass after all."

He'd said that he loved her. And she'd said that she loved him. Had either one of them been telling the truth?

"Look," she said, trying to keep her voice light as she pointed toward where the sun was beginning to sink on the horizon. "It's going to be a gorgeous sunset."

"They always are, down here."

She turned toward him suddenly, looking at him with an intensity that startled him, searching his eyes, her face just a little wild. Rafe wanted to reach out and take hold of her hand, reassure her somehow, but he wasn't sure why. What was she asking of him? Before he could figure it out, she'd turned away and was racing along the sand again.

"I'm starving," she called back over her shoulder. "And I don't have any money with me. Could you treat me to dinner?"

"Treat you to dinner?"

She made a face. "Don't worry. I'll pay you back."

"That's not what worries me."

But she wasn't listening. She'd fixed a large, glass-enclosed structure that sprawled out on the beach before them in her sights. "I want a huge, glorious dinner with broiled lobster and crisp sourdough rolls and thick sweet butter, asparagus tips, Death by Chocolate cake...."

Rafe followed where her gaze was leading. One of Marina del Rey's most exclusive hotels. He pointed. "That looks like the sort of restaurant where you can probably get all that and more."

She stopped and turned back to look at him in the face, her own alive with anticipation. "Well?"

He smiled back at her. He couldn't help it. There was something contagious about her enthusiasm. He wanted to do little things to make her happy, make her light up the air with that smile. "Let's go," he said.

The maître d' took a deep breath, his wide eyes taking in Kendall's disheveled gown and her bare feet, from which she brushed vast quantities of sand. Then she slipped back into her shoes, which Rafe presented and she accepted as though they were gifts he'd dived for in the deep. It was evident that this was highly irregular. The maître d' blanched a bit, examining the rest of her appearance, the flushed face, the wrinkled garment, the little hat slightly askew, its veil twisted around her neck to keep it out of the way.

"Perhaps mademoiselle . . . uh . . . madame . . . would like to change into her traveling suit before dinner?" he suggested tactfully.

"Traveling suit?" Kendall looked up at him, her face innocently blank.

He coughed discreetly into his soft, curled hand. "Are you not about to embark on your honeymoon trip?" he asked knowingly.

She laughed, white teeth flashing. "Oh, heavens, no. We're going to honeymoon right here in your restaurant. Aren't we?" she asked Rafe, slipping her arm through his and grinning up at him impudently. "Just show us to a table, please, so we can get started."

The maître d' looked shocked, then gazed about helplessly. It was apparent he had never encountered this situation before and wasn't sure what to do. This was a staid and proper restaurant. He didn't want to create a stir.

"Don't worry," Kendall told him in a stage whisper, her eyes dancing. "We're sane. Believe me. It's okay."

He could no more resist her wide smile than could Rafe. Surrendering, the man nodded. "This way, please," he said in a strangled voice.

Kendall tripped along behind him, oblivious to the startled stares that greeted her along the way.

Rafe, following, caught them all. It was still early and the restaurant wasn't crowded.

The maître d' seated them at a table away from the main floor, at a huge window overlooking the ocean. A waiter appeared with menus, did a double take at Kendall and retired, smiling nervously.

"What is the problem with everyone?" Kendall asked innocently. "I feel like a freak in a carnival exhibit."

Rafe sat back in his chair and grunted, scowling to keep his grin from surfacing. "The thing is, brides usually do not eat in restaurants in full regalia."

"Ah, but there we have it, the point of the whole matter. I'm not a bride, am I?"

"Sure you are. Well..."

Kendall nodded wisely, working hard to keep the pain at bay. "Almost a bride, that's all. All image and no substance." Her eyes took on a faraway look. "It would have been fun, you know." Her voice sounded very small. "It was fun. Just for a while."

Without thinking, Rafe reached across the table and covered her hand with his own. It was an uncharacteristic move on his part, and it startled him that he'd done it. But he left his hand there. Her skin felt smooth, silky, and he wanted to ring her wrist with his fingers and pull her toward him.

She didn't pull away. She turned her dark eyes to him with a vague sense of curiosity, waiting for him to say something. He felt her waiting, and he didn't know what to say to her.

But before he could speak, a short, cheerful-looking waitress bustled up to the table and gave a delighted cackle. "Just married, huh? Oh, how cute!" She beamed at them both, disregarding their dismayed looks as they jerked their hands apart. "Oh, anyone could tell, even if you didn't still have on your wedding gown. You've got that dewy look, the two of you. You'll need champagne, now, won't you? This is certainly the time to celebrate. I'm Molly. I'll be right back." She was off again without waiting for an answer.

Kendall looked at Rafe and laughed. "I don't know, what do you think? Are we the perfect couple or what?"

His answering smile was more perfunctory than she had expected. "Are you married?" she asked with sudden insight.

But he shook his head. "I was once."

She nodded slowly, reading the signs. "Not a good experience, huh? That makes us both unlucky at love." Her irrepressible smile was back. "Hey, who knows? Maybe this is fate. Maybe we've been thrown together for a reason."

He didn't smile back, and the shadows that clouded his eyes surprised her.

The waitress returned with a bucket of ice and a huge bottle of champagne, chortling as she set the glasses down and reached for the bottle. "The two of you look adorable together. Made for each other, that's what."

The bottle came open with a pop that made Kendall jump and giggle.

"You'll have a lovely life together, mark my words." The waitress patted Kendall's shoulder as she poured out a bit of the golden liquid for Rafe to taste. "Church wedding?" she asked.

"Chapel," Kendall said, looking back in her mind's eye. "It was lovely. The place was crammed with tulips and irises."

"Oh! Tulips. My favorite." Tears seemed to be coming to Molly's hazel eyes. "And when I think of my wedding, in a dusty New Mexico tavern with flies on the bar..." She shook her head sorrowfully. "You're lucky, honey. Believe me, cherish this guy."

Rafe cocked an eyebrow Kendall's way as the waitress hurried off. "Don't you think you're carrying this a bit too far?" he asked mildly.

She grinned at him. "Listen, we gals have to take our romances as we find them," she said.

His piercing gaze seemed to cut right through her. "The next thing you're going to want is our portrait painted on black velvet."

Kendall's mouth dropped open at the sheer genius of it all. "What a great idea. Just the two of us, to commemorate this day."

He drew back, as though he were almost afraid she might mean it. "Sorry," he said more shortly than was absolutely necessary. "I'm not available for portraits."

She sighed and sipped at her champagne. She'd been kidding. He didn't have to get that look of panic on his face. It only made that dull feeling of dread in her stomach throb a little more sharply. Why was it that men backed away from her? It seemed to be a trend. Lately, most men she met got a wary look in their eyes as she became friendlier. Darren had caught the look-out-for-Kendall flu late in the game, but he seemed to have a terminal case. And now Rafe was looking nervous. What was it? Did she come on too strong? Or just too needy?

She shuddered. If there was anything she wanted to avoid, it was to come across as needy. She could take care of herself.

Molly was back, ready to take their order, and Kendall chose lobster, just as she'd said she would. Rafe ordered a salmon fillet with a salad. The waitress jokingly asked if he wanted oysters, thinking she would make them both laugh. Instead, her little joke was met with stony silence on both sides.

"Uh, any appetizers at all?" she ventured, looking worried.

"I'd like the tiger prawns," Kendall offered with a sly look at Rafe. "With two forks."

"Oh, good." Molly looked relieved at this sign that all was well in honeymoon land. She refilled Kendall's empty champagne glass. "You two should toast your future. How many kids are you aiming for?"

"Half a dozen at least," Kendall said promptly. "We both love kids. Don't we, honey?"

Rafe glared, and she grinned.

"Well, that's just fine," Molly babbled on as she set out their salads. "And your children will have his blue eyes and your auburn hair...."

"Oh, no." Kendall broke in with a bland smile as she emptied her glass. "I want blondes with green eyes."

"Blondes?" The woman looked slightly taken aback.

Kendall nodded happily. "I've always wanted blond kids."

Molly looked worried. Her glance went from Rafe to Kendall, and then back again. She bent close to Kendall, as though her words were for the bride alone. "Then, honey, I'm sorry, but I think you married the wrong guy." She gave Rafe a furtive look. "You should have married a blond fella."

Kendall took a long, long sip of champagne, staring hard at Rafe, then blinked. "Doggone. You're right. Why didn't I think of that?" She looked up at the waitress. "What should I do?"

Molly was beginning to get suspicious. She sniffed, folding up her order pad. "Either set your sights on brunettes," she said evenly, "or start making plans for adoption." She turned, shaking her head, and hurried away.

Kendall gave Rafe a look of great regret. "I guess we're not really the perfect couple after all," she said sadly. "Too bad, isn't it?"

"You're going to have to stop this," Rafe told her calmly. "You're driving everyone crazy."

"Including you?"

"Mostly me."

She studied him over the rim of her glass. The champagne was making her light-headed. That must have been why he was beginning to look so darkly dangerous, like a certain Transylvanian count or a Western gunslinger. Suddenly she shivered. What did she actually know about him anyway? Hadn't it been just a little foolhardy to put herself in his hands and in his debt this way? This was a crazy time to trust any man. She'd just been kicked in the teeth. She was at her most vulnerable ever.

And in the next sixty seconds, she proved it.

She heard a voice, glanced up and saw the back of a head—and there was Darren. He'd shown up after all! What a relief. He was going to explain it all away and...

"Darren!" She jumped up from the table and started toward him, laughing, looking down at Rafe as if to say, "See, you thought he'd dumped me, but you were wrong." She turned back toward the room. "Darren, over here!"

Rafe rose, too, turned and caught her arm.

"That's not Darren, Kendall," he said harshly.

She pulled at his grip, angry with him. "Yes, it is. Look, he's..."

The man turned and looked at her oddly. Rafe was right. It wasn't Darren. A quiver of loss tore through her, and she slumped back against Rafe. "Oh."

Rafe's arm came around her, hard and protective. She looked out at the crowd. Faces everywhere were turned toward her, gazing impassively. Not only was the crazy lady in a wedding gown, now she was attempting to accost strangers. What a scene. Kendall wanted to shrink back into the warmth of the arms around her, but she steeled herself, lifted her chin and smiled at them all. Then she turned grandly and sat back down in her chair.

Rafe stood over her. "Are you all right?" he asked softly.

She nodded, not looking up. "Sure. I'm as all right as any other circus freak who's just been rejected," she muttered, picking at her salad, not really hungry any longer.

He tried to look into her eyes, but she was busy examining the salad. "Is it really bothering you? Being in a place like this in a wedding dress, I mean."

She shrugged, smiling at him faintly. "I don't see that I have much choice, unless I want to go hungry."

He stared at her for a moment, then came to a decision. Throwing down his napkin, he turned. "Stay here. I'm going to go buy you a dress."

Her eyes widened. "What?"

"We passed a number of little dress shops in the lobby as we came in. What size are you? What color do you like?"

Laughing, she reached to catch hold of his hand. "No, really, you don't have to do this."

He looked down at her, pulling away from her touch. "Don't go away."

"Oh, sure. Where would I go?"

Suddenly he hesitated, looking back at her. What if she did go away? His hand tightened on the back of the chair, and then he mentally kicked himself. What did he care if she did go away? If she wanted to go, it was her business. But she'd said herself she had no money. And she was very hungry. She would stay.

"I'll be right back," he said.

"Rafe..."

She watched him go, a bemused smile still softening her face. Despite what he'd said, he was being awfully nice. Even if it was just out of pity. She remembered how she had been comparing him to Dracula just a few moments before and laughed softly. She was vulnerable right now. Her emotions were in a tailspin. She had better be careful or she might do or say something she was really going to regret.

Rafe was no expert at buying women's clothes. He looked at the mannequins in the boutique and pointed. "That one," he said, selecting a red dress that looked like something one of Darren's girlfriends would wear. He had no idea if Kendall would like it.

Waiting with his credit card in hand, he smiled to himself. He'd forgotten how much fun it was to buy a gift for a woman. Especially a woman like Kendall, someone open and responsive, who didn't try to hide her every thought behind a sneer. She was going to like this. As long as she was still there when he got back.

She was an odd one, hard to figure out. Whenever he thought he'd seen her true feelings in her eyes, she seemed to change. He'd almost decided that she *wasn't* really devastated by what had happened to her today. Then she'd mistaken that stranger for Darren and for just a moment, every bit of her pain had been mirrored on her face, there for all to see.

She was hurt, all right. At some point that hurt was going to turn to anger. And that thought made Rafe pause. His smile faded. What would she say if she knew he was the one who had told Darren he didn't have to marry her after all?

She wasn't going to leave. Even so, he found himself hurrying to get back to her, just in case.

Kendall flushed with pleasure when he handed her the bag, just as he had known she would, looking up almost shyly. "I'll go put it on in the rest room," she said. Rising from the table, she stopped to drop a kiss on his cheek. "Thanks, Rafe," she said softly, her eyes shining. "I really, really appreciate it."

Her appreciation lasted until she'd slipped the dress over her head, tugged it into place and looked at herself in the mirror. She blinked, then frowned, her shoulders sagging. What was this, a joke? Well, okay. She supposed she could go along with it.

Ripping pins out, she let her hair swing free, down to where it bounced against her bottom. She stuffed as much as she could of the wedding gown into the plastic bag the dress had come in and started back to the table, marching with new determination. And this time, she noticed the looks she got as she went. If she hadn't been so annoyed, she might have blushed.

Rafe looked up and saw her coming. His smile was guileless. She faltered for a moment. Was it possible he didn't realize what he'd done? Plunking the bag in the empty chair, she stepped back and posed, watching his eyes.

"Do you like it?"

He examined her for a long, long moment, not sure what she was getting at, but enjoying the transformation. She had looked ethereally beautiful in the wedding gown, but this was more earthy, a real, flesh-and-blood seduction of a woman. The muscles of his abdomen tightened as his gaze lingered on the way the red fabric stretched taut across her full breasts, the way her hips jutted out against the gathered Lycra fabric. Her body was drop-dead fantastic. The blood in his veins was beating wild agreement.

"Yes," he said at last, just a little hoarse. "You look very good."

He didn't notice that her eyes flared at his words. She slipped into her chair and leaned toward him, her smile frosty. "Of course, I do. This dress is made to make a woman look good." The smile turned into an icy glare. "Every self-respecting streetwalker should have one."

He'd finally begun to realize that she wasn't pleased, but why, he couldn't imagine. "What, you think it's a little too—"

"Yes, exactly. It's a little 'too.'" She looked down at her generously exposed cleavage and shuddered, giving the neckline a tug to pull it up for at least a bit of coverage. "A little 'too' just about everything."

He frowned, like a man just trying to get things straight. "You mean you don't usually wear clothes like this?"

She sighed and tapped her fingers against the table-cloth, a woman dealing with a slow male intellect, and spoke clearly and precisely, just to make sure. "I usually wear jeans and an old sweatshirt—when I'm not in a swimsuit. A one-piece, very utilitarian swimsuit, often accessorized by a big old towel with a faded picture of James Dean wrapped around my waist. I don't spend too much time on street corners. I run a swim school, you know," she said almost as an aside.

He blinked. "You run your own business?" he repeated blankly. He was getting it. He was finally getting it. He'd made a very dumb mistake, a silly assumption. Yes, he could see now that this dress was not her style at all. It was the style of the woman Sam had told him about the night before. But that woman seemed to have less and less to do with the Kendall Rafe was getting to know.

Still, the dress did look good on her. It showed off attributes a man couldn't help but admire. And Rafe couldn't help but glance at them once again.

"I don't know, I just assumed—"

"You assumed wrong."

He nodded slowly, searching her eyes. "I'm sorry, Kendall. I just don't know that much about women's clothes. It looked like a pretty dress to me. I really didn't mean any harm. Want me to take it back?"

She met his gaze for a long moment, then sighed, softening. He was sincere, as far as she could tell. All she'd really wanted was an acknowledgement, and now she had it.

"No," she said, settling back. "I can stand it. Although, I'll tell you what—I was more comfortable with the stares when I was wearing the wedding gown than I am in this."

Pulling her napkin onto her lap, she prepared to attack the huge lobster that had appeared at her place while she was gone. Her appetite was coming back.

He watched her, bemused. She was a real, vibrant, intelligent woman. What the hell had she been doing with his brother? "You're better off without him, you know," he said suddenly.

She looked up and nodded. "Oh, I know. I've known that for a long time."

Rafe's dark eyebrows drew together. This was where it all fell apart for him. For some reason, he had to know the truth, settle this, put it in its proper cubby-hole in his mind so he could accept it. "Then why were you going to marry him?"

She waved her fork and considered, her dark eyes narrowing thoughtfully. "That's a toughy. Do you really want to know?"

"Yes." He leaned forward. At this moment, it was imperative that he find out.

She took a bite of the tender white meat, savored it with a look of ecstasy, swallowed with a happy sigh and went on. "We met in a scuba class."

"You were taking scuba lessons?"

"No. I was teaching them."

Yes, that would fit with the way he was beginning to see the relationship shaping up. Darren was his brother, and he had some family feeling for him, but Darren was a player in the game of life, not a master. He took classes. He took trips. He even took jobs. But he never taught or managed or directed anything. Kendall, on the other hand...

"Darren was taking the lessons," she continued. "He was such a klutz." A bemused smile tickled the corners of her mouth and lit her eyes as she remembered. "There was no way I would ever let him go down alone. I had to stick by him at all times to make sure he would come back alive." She shrugged, reaching for her wine goblet. "But he made me laugh. He took me to Catalina on a yacht. We had so much fun." She sipped from her glass, remembering, and shook her head.

"Then we played phone tag for a couple of weeks. I was so busy—and I wasn't sure I wanted to get involved. But you know, he didn't give up like most men would have. He kept trying to find me, to pin me down to another date. So I went out with him again. I figured it would just peter out—like all those things do lately.''

Her eyes darkened as that thought came to her, and she glanced at Rafe, wondering what he was like in a relationship. "Most of the men I've dated recently are not exactly in the market for lasting commitments. When you get to be my age, the men who are interested are usually divorced. They've been married and they don't particularly want a repeat yet. They just want to have some fun for a while and move on." She stared at the ocean and went on in a soft voice, almost to herself. "It gets really lonely sometimes. You sort of feel like just another way station along the road to the ideal California bachelor life-style."

Hearing the maudlin tone beginning to take hold in her own voice, she looked at Rafe quickly and grinned, trying to get back the lightness. "I began to feel like my front yard was a graveyard of expired relationships," she quipped. "One after another, the things faded away or dropped dead on my doorstep." She shrugged again, pushing her heavy hair back over her shoulder. "You start to ask yourself, is it me? Is it this crazy time we live in? Am I just meeting the wrong men? What is it?"

She stopped for a moment, contemplating what she'd just said. It was getting more and more difficult to focus. She knew she was drinking too much champagne. She would have to cut it out. But the golden liquid was making things feel pleasantly fuzzy. Still, she wanted to get this right, really let him know how she had ended up with Darren, what it was like for her.

She glanced at Rafe. She'd left herself wide open to comment, but so far, he hadn't offered an opinion. She went on, still explaining, trying to make him see, because she could sense he was really puzzled. "I was beginning to feel like I was losing it with relationships. But all of a sudden, there was Darren. He was so much fun. And then, a miracle." She glanced at Rafe again, waiting to see his reaction. "He wanted to get married."

Rafe's face was hard. If he was filled with understanding and compassion, he sure didn't show it. And neither did the tone of his skeptical voice.

"So you said you would marry him just because he was the only one who'd asked lately?"

Kendall abandoned the lobster and clutched her champagne. Rafe was obviously determined to be difficult about this, but she wasn't going to let him get her goat. "No." She glared at him defiantly. "But he was the only one I had been in love with. *That* had something to do with it." She settled herself down, and added with more conviction, "Besides, he was fun to be with."

Rafe was staring at her, examining every nuance in detail. "Yeah," he said with soft sarcasm. "A real fun guy."

"Well, he was. I can't help it. I hadn't been having much fun." She took a deep breath and went a little further. "Being with Darren made me realize how dull my life had become. We had a good time together. He made me happy." She searched Rafe's eyes for one hint of compassion. "I want to be happy," she said softly. "Is that a crime?"

Rafe grimaced, almost as though with pain. His blue eyes flickered with something that wasn't sympathy, but came close. "No, Kendall," he said huskily, looking at her, "that is not a crime."

It wasn't a lot, but it was better than nothing. She took another long drink of champagne and suddenly her glass was empty. Staring at it for a moment, she looked about the table for more. Molly had brought another bottle, and when Kendall held her glass out, Rafe filled it for her yet again, hardly noticing what he was doing, his mind absorbed with her, with what she'd been telling him.

A sick feeling was taking over the pit of his stomach. He was beginning to admit to himself that something ghastly had happened. He'd made a horrible mistake. No matter how he tried to rationalize it, telling Darren he didn't have to marry Kendall had been wrong.

It had seemed so simple. Darren was a playboy, completely unmarriageable. Kendall McCormick was supposed to be one of his usual bimbos who was using pregnancy to trap Darren into a marriage that was doomed from the start—a marriage Darren didn't really want, a marriage he could never handle. Big brother had stepped in, consoled poor Darren, told him to tell the girl to take a hike. Big brother would go on over and do the dirty work, pick up the pieces, pay her off or whatever it took. God, he must have been living in some sort of cartoon world while all that was going on.

But cartoons had a way of turning on you, of ending much too fast. And now big brother had been confronted with reality.

Kendall was no bimbo. She was a beautiful, capable woman who would make any man a wonderful wife. In fact, Kendall might be the best thing that ever happened to Darren. What had he done here? Rafe wondered.

"I've got to make a phone call," he said suddenly, throwing down his napkin. "Don't go away."

She smiled at him dreamily, holding the glass of champagne in the air. "Where would I go?" she replied, her words slightly slurred.

He stared at her in horror, finally realizing what was going on. She was pregnant and he had sat here, watching her drink for an hour now and not thought a thing about it. Lord, was there no end to the stupid things he was capable of today?

Reaching out like a man saving a lady from a striking snake, he slipped the glass from her fingers and threw it and its contents into a bank of potted plants behind her seat, while she stared at him blankly.

"You can't drink alcohol," he barked at her sternly. "Don't you know that? Not in your condition. Haven't you read all the latest studies?"

Her eyes widened. "My condition?" Frowning, she tried indignation with only marginal success. "Listen, you, I'm not drunk. I'm not hardly drunk at all. What are you talking about?"

But he had already taken the bottle from the table and jabbed it back into the ice bucket.

"Stay away from that stuff," he ordered. "I'll be right back."

Kendall stared after him. Her mind was getting very foggy now, and she couldn't quite grasp what was going on here. She wanted champagne. She liked champagne. So she was a little tipsy. If anyone had a right to get soused tonight, it was her. Who did he think he was anyway, her father?

Hah. She would show him a thing or two. Pushing herself up out of her chair, Kendall lurched forward and retrieved the bottle, then sank back and smiled. She would drink if she darn well felt like it. Slowly, carefully, with delicate finesse, she tipped the bottle to her lips.

The phone rang twenty-two times before Rafe gave up. Darren wasn't home. Rafe had to track him down and reverse the mistake he'd made. If he had to grab Darren by the neck and prop him up before the preacher with a shotgun, he'd do it. Kendall deserved at least that much.

But Darren was going to be elusive. He'd been out like a light when Rafe had left him that afternoon. Surely he couldn't have gone too far. Quickly, Rafe went through a list of possibilities and made a decision, leading him back to the telephone. To his surprise, information did have Sam's number. It only rang once before Sam answered.

"Where the hell is Darren?" he demanded, almost snarling.

Sam stammered, "D-D-Darren? Oh, is this Rafe?"

"Where the hell is my brother?"

"Gone. Darren's gone."

"Gone?" Ice filled Rafe's veins. "What do you mean 'gone'?"

"Well, you know, he had tickets for Hawaii for the honeymoon. He cashed them in for a one-way to Australia. His visa was still good from—"

"You let him go?"

"Why not? His plane left about an hour ago. Listen, how did the chick take the news?"

Rafe's knuckles were white from his death grip on the receiver. "Kendall McCormick is no chick, you bastard. Do you realize you may have ruined this woman's life?"

"Me?" Sam's familiar whine was strong in his voice. "I didn't do anything."

Rafe closed his eyes for a moment, steadying himself. Sam was right. He hadn't done anything but babble his gossipy innuendoes, something he had done for years on end, something Rafe knew very well he did. It was Rafe who had talked to Darren. It was Rafe who had given his brother an okay. It was Rafe who had gone blithely to the chapel to tell Kendall that the man she loved, the father of her child, had turned his back on her. He couldn't get away with blaming this on Sam. Rafe licked his dry lips. "When's Darren going to be back?"

"Rafe, didn't you hear what I told you? He bought a one-way ticket. He's thinking of emigrating."

Rafe swore softly and obscenely. "Did he give you an address? Any way to get in touch with him?"

"Nope. Sorry." Sam's voice changed, sounding more whining all the time. "What is it, Rafe? What's the matter? You agreed he should get out of this marriage thing."

Rafe took a deep breath. "I was wrong, Sam," he growled. "And so were you."

He slammed down the phone and turned to go back, steeling himself for what he was going to have to do. This had become his mess. He was going to have to deal with it.

Three

Currently, the "mess" consisted of Kendall sitting with her legs drawn up under her in her chair, humming as she polished off the champagne, her lobster cold and forgotten before her.

"Hi," she said, looking at Rafe drowsily as he returned to the table. "You're a swell guy, you know that?" She leaned toward him, smiling, overcome by a wave of affection. "A really swell guy. I wish I could marry a swell guy like you. You wouldn't run away like Darren, would you?"

"Kendall," Rafe said harshly as he slipped back into his seat, "you're bombed."

She shook her head resolutely, her thick chocolate hair swirling around her face. "S'impossible. I don't drink."

He held up the empty bottle and glared at her. "What do you think this is, lemonade?"

"S'champagne." She smiled happily. "S'good stuff." A frown caught hold of her eyebrows, and she tried hard to be serious. "Champagne's okay. S'my wedding day. I can have it." She nodded hard, just to make sure he got the point.

He stared at her, at a loss. She was damn adorable—and damn infuriating at the same time. What was he going to do with her? He couldn't very well drive her home along the freeways in his open sports car in this condition. There was only one solution. He'd have to book her a room here in the hotel for the night.

"Let's go," he said, throwing a few large bills onto the table.

She stared at him, trying hard to understand. "Go?"

He nodded, looking at the way her hair was falling over her eyes, resisting the temptation to smooth it back. "I'm going to put you to bed."

Her eyes sparkled. "Ooh." She shivered deliciously.

He wasn't sure what that reaction meant, and he wasn't sure he wanted to know. But she looked so fragile, so lost, he reached out and took her hand in his.

"I know it's been a rough day, Kendall," he said softly. "I'm...I'm really sorry. In a way, you deserve to get as plastered as you feel like getting. But...you can't do things like this. It isn't good for the baby."

"The baby?" Her eyes widened and she looked around groggily. "Where?"

His hand tightened on hers. "Come on. Let's get you a room."

She straightened her legs and tried to stand, wobbling on her heels.

"Oops." Reaching out, she grabbed him for support.

"Come on." His arm came around her, protective, comforting, and she relaxed into it, smiling up at him in a way that made him wince and look away. "Come on, you can do it."

"I'm trying," she protested, clutching his arms and giggling. "I'm just a little itsy bitsy tipsy."

He drew her closer, feeling something warm swell inside him. She felt soft and breakable at the same time. She needed him. He wanted to protect her from the world. Glancing around the room at the curious faces, he glared defensively and led her away.

She made it through the registration process in a fairly coherent state, but by the time they got to the elevators, she'd had it. Her legs had turned to rubber, and she couldn't quite make out where she was supposed to put her feet.

Giving up after the third time she'd slumped against him, Rafe looked around to make sure they didn't have much of an audience, and, after handing her the bag with the wedding gown drooling out of it, reached his hands around her small waist and swung her up over his shoulder. And there he stood, waiting for the elevator.

She didn't say anything at first, didn't make a move. He almost thought she might have fallen asleep. But just before the elevator arrived, she cleared her throat and spoke, making him cringe, her voice loud and clear enough to carry to San Diego. "Rafe, why are you carrying me?"

Looking around quickly, with a defiant glance at the growing crowd of onlookers, he answered in a hoarse whisper, hoping to quiet her. "Because you're drunk."

The elevator arrived and the door opened to disgorge a dozen people, just in time to hear Kendall disclaim at the top of her lungs, "I'm not drunk. Drunk people sing songs."

Double takes were the order of the day as the people filed by. Meanwhile, there was a pause as that thought was carefully digested by Kendall's foggy mind.

"Hey Rafe, you want to sing a song with me?" Suddenly that seemed a supremely excellent idea. She raised her head and tried to turn to where she could get a look at his face. "What'll we sing?"

"We're not singing," he whispered through clenched teeth. Clutching her legs, he swung onto the elevator, avoiding the startled stares of the middle-aged man and woman who had stayed aboard.

"Okay. I'll just wave to people." Kendall turned back and looked out into the lobby of the hotel just before the door closed. "Hi, people," she called, trying to wave.

The doors slammed shut before anyone could answer, leaving Rafe and Kendall alone with the middle-aged couple. Disapproval was thick as peanut butter in the tiny compartment.

Kendall raised her head again and smiled at the female face she could barely make out. "Hi," she said dreamily.

The woman pursed her lips suspiciously. "Hello, dear," she said shortly, casting Rafe a vicious glare. "Are you all right?"

Kendall smiled her wide, beatific smile. "I'm fine. Rafe is taking such good care of me."

"Is he, indeed?" The woman's small black eyes snapped, and she stepped around to where she could come face-to-face with Rafe.

"Sir," she demanded smartly. "What are you doing to this young woman?"

Rafe sighed. He could have done without this. They were almost to the room. Today, he didn't have any luck at all. "Listen, I know how this looks—"

The woman had no patience for his excuses. "I'll tell you how it looks. It looks as though you've inebriated this lovely girl until all her good judgment has flown out the window, and now you are proceeding to carry her off to your room, where you are planning to do God knows what to her."

Rafe groaned and shifted Kendall to a better position. "No, it's not like that. Listen . . ."

But in the shift, Kendall had let go of the bag she was carrying, and she strained around to find help. "Oops." She tried to get a look at the helpful woman who was talking to Rafe. "Could you pick up my wedding gown, please? I dropped it."

The woman turned her attention to the bag on the floor. Half the wedding gown had spilled out of it. She blinked in surprise.

"Please hand it to me," Kendall suggested, waving her arm about with her hand open. "Thank you."

The woman picked up the bag and stared at its contents. "Wedding gown?" she said, aghast. "My dear, have you just been married?"

Kendall was trying to be coherent, but it wasn't easy. The room wouldn't stand still. "Did you come to my wedding?" she asked, squinting, trying to bring the woman's face into focus. "Sorry it was a flop. I'll give you back your present, honest."

The elevator shuddered to a stop and the doors opened. Unfortunately, it seemed both couples were getting off on the same floor. Rafe glanced quickly at the directory, getting his bearings, hoping to make a quick getaway. But the woman with the sparkling black eyes seemed to have formed an attachment to Kendall. She walked right alongside them.

"You should be ashamed of yourself," she said in a low voice to Rafe as they walked. "How could you do this to your bride on your wedding night? How could you let her get herself in this position?"

Kendall's head came up again. "It's a good position. I can watch feet from here. And I can wave at the people." She demonstrated to the empty corridor.

The woman grunted in distaste. "How could you do this to the woman that you love?" she demanded of Rafe.

"Oh, it's okay," Kendall offered, craning to try to see them both. "He doesn't love me."

Shock turned the woman's face gray. "What?"

"No, really, we don't love each other. So it's okay."

The woman looked from one to the other, shaken, as Rafe stopped before a door, fumbling for the key and hurrying as fast as he could to get Kendall into the room and find a little privacy.

"Why would you marry a man you don't love, my dear?" the woman was asking Kendall.

Kendall was ready to spill her life story out before the world as Rafe worked with the key. "Oh, you see, the man I thought I loved didn't show up for the wedding." She shook her head sadly. "I was jilted. So I found Rafe and I ran away."

The key worked. The door was open. Rafe breathed a sigh of relief and swung Kendall to the floor. Her legs weren't about to support her, so he had to make a quick grab to hold her upright, but she hardly seemed to notice. She was still talking to the nosy woman.

"It's a long story. A very long story." Kendall brightened with a new idea, and as Rafe tried to pull her into the room, she turned back to the woman. "Why don't you come on in and have a drink and I'll tell you all about it?" she suggested groggily. "Do we have any more champagne?"

The woman looked on the point of taking Kendall up on it, but Rafe intervened. "Another time," he said firmly, smiling and closing the door in the woman's face.

"But...I was going to tell her about my wedding," Kendall protested.

Frustration finally took its toll, and Rafe answered harshly, "You didn't have a wedding, remember?" He immediately regretted his words as her huge, dark eyes widened, then filled with tears.

"Kendall..." He hesitated, looking at her. That warm feeling was swelling inside him again, and he was afraid if he touched her...

But he had very little choice in the matter. She was swaying toward him and he reached out, steadying her with hands on her shoulders, trying to keep his distance. But her hands stretched out toward him, fingers curling around the lapels of his shirt, and before he could stop himself, his arms wrapped around her, drawing her against his chest.

"I'm sorry," he whispered into the perfumed darkness of her hair. "Kendall, I— I'm really sorry."

Sorry for putting her in this position, sorry for being such a jerk, sorry for letting her get drunk, sorry for everything.

She was sobbing, clutching him, and he stroked her hair, wishing he knew what to do to comfort her. She felt so good in his arms. He murmured things, and when she turned her face up to his, he let his lips linger against her temple. She tasted sweet and smelled even better. His mouth moved, and before he knew what he was doing, he was kissing the soft area in front of her ear.

He pulled himself back, swearing softly. This was no good. She was a lovely, tempting package, but he wasn't a damn teenager. He could resist temptation. He was going to get her to bed and get himself out of here.

He swung her up into his arms and she went limp against him. Good. She'd had a good cry and now she was ready to sleep. He carried her to the bed, which was already turned down, and dropped her carefully onto the cool sheets.

She lay back, eyes closed, and he stood for a moment, watching her breathe. How could Darren have turned his back on this? The idiot didn't deserve her.

He considered leaving her in the red dress, but quickly thought better of it. The stupid thing was too tight—another one of his mistakes of the day. He'd better get it off her.

Hesitating, he steeled himself. He was a grown man. He'd been married. He'd had his share of women. He had no need to undress a helpless woman in order to get kicks. He would do this quickly, with detached, surgical precision.

Ignoring the wave of scent that came his way as he turned her, he reached for the zipper at the back of the dress, brushing aside her thick hair, and pulled it down quickly. The top of the dress came apart easily, and he avoided looking at what it revealed. The fabric was still stretched tightly across the hips, and he had to tug and yank to get it down, turning her gently as he did.

And then the dress was in his hands and he threw it onto the chair and turned back to cover her. But one look at her lovely body and he was paralyzed, stopped as though someone had slugged him hard in the solar plexus.

She was beautiful. Her hair cascaded about her like water down a cliff, framing a face that was angelic in sleep. Her skin was smooth, tan fading to a pearly white at her breasts. The filmy ivory bra cups were filled and revealed flat dark nipples that looked butter smooth through the lace. She looked athletic, her waist small, her hips wide, her stomach flat, not showing any hint of the pregnancy. Her legs were long and strong, her toenails a shimmering pink.

It took an effort to start breathing again. He reached to cover her, but somehow his hand detoured along the way to cup her shoulder and run along the smooth, silky length of her arm. Her skin felt the way roses smelled. His stomach seemed to fall away, and something began to ache in his chest. Rafe had to jerk his hand away and force himself to reach for the covers, drawing them up over her and tucking her in.

Then he stood for a long time, staring down at the curve of her cheek, the tousled hair. He wasn't really thinking. He was just standing there, pulling himself together.

Finally he turned and went to the telephone, dialing the desk.

"I'd like to order a car for the morning," he said, pulling out his credit card. "Put it in my name. But a Ms. McCormick will be picking it up." As he talked, he jotted down a note, explaining to Kendall that she had a car waiting for her.

That done, he extracted several twenties from his wallet and laid them next to the note. As he began to shove the wallet back into his pocket, a sound came from the bed.

Turning quickly, he found her sitting up, rubbing her eyes as though she'd just woken from a long sleep.

"Rafe?" She looked bewildered.

He went to her quickly, gently lowering her back down on the pillow.

"Get some sleep, Kendall," he said softly, stroking her cheek with the back of his hand.

She was tired, her eyelids drooping, but she smiled, and suddenly her arms came up around him, her fingers sliding into his hair, tugging him closer.

"The room is spinning," she whispered. "Hold me."

"No, Kendall...."

But he was already bending toward her even as the words evaporated into the air. She was pulling him toward temptation, and it was getting harder and harder to resist.

She strained to meet him, her body alive beneath him, taut as a cord about to break. He hesitated one more time, just before his lips touched hers.

"Kendall, no. You need to sleep."

"I need you to hold me."

He was right and she was wrong, and he knew it. But her mouth claimed his and he wasn't that strong a man. With a groan, he abandoned chivalry and took what she was offering, took her wildness and her heat and caressed it, held it close, plunged into the heart of it and reveled in its pleasure.

She tasted like dawn, felt like firelight, smelled like yellow roses. She was more than a woman. She was passion and danger and things that were always just out of reach. He wanted her, and she scared him. He couldn't have her, but he could have this for just a moment....

Her hands had found their way beneath his shirt and were sliding up his bare chest, making him writhe and groan. "Love me, Rafe," she said softly, urgently. "I need you. Love me."

He felt heavy, drugged, as though he were sleep-walking. He knew he should pull away, but he couldn't do it. Her touch was like fire on his skin. He had to kiss her, let his lips caress her face, let his tongue find where she was most sensitive. He felt her legs twisting around his, pulling him closer, tighter, drawing him into the cradle of her hips.

She was more responsive than any woman he had ever been with. His kiss made her move against the sheets, his touch made her gasp and reach for him. Need for her was beginning to beat like a war drum in his body.

He didn't want to stop. But he knew this was insane. This was the woman Darren was supposed to marry. She didn't really want him. All she was looking for was another drug, like champagne, to ease her hurt. He couldn't take advantage of her vulnerability like this. And most of all, he couldn't make love with the woman who was carrying his brother's child.

That was the thought that froze him, gave him the strength to pull away from her and stop what had begun so quickly and furiously.

The woman who was carrying his brother's child. What was wrong with him? How could he have even thought about her this way, much less acted upon those thoughts?

Rafe drew back slowly, hardening himself to her soft cries of disappointment. Pulling a chair up beside the bed, he sat down and began to stroke her hair, talking to her softly, mostly saying nonsense things, anything to quiet her. She murmured something he couldn't understand, but her eyes began to close, and pretty soon she was asleep.

He sat stroking her for almost an hour more, watching her breathe, trying to make sense out of what had almost happened. It was crazy. And yet he couldn't truthfully say he was sorry. The one thing he could do was make a promise to himself that it would never happen again.

Four

"This doesn't look very much like Hawaii."

Kendall said the words aloud, talking to the air. It was the first thought that tiptoed into her quaking mind as she woke up in the strange room, gazing about at the heavy brocades and velveteens. And things went downhill from there.

She wasn't married, was she? That truth blinked at her like a gaudy neon sign. Darren hadn't even had the guts to face her with his decision. Pain shot through her with a jagged shock of electricity once she came to the full realization. No marriage. No Darren. The fact that he'd only proved he wasn't worth all the trouble was beside the point, and cold comfort, as well. It still hurt like anything.

Other people met someone, fell in love, got married, had children, lived normal lives. What was wrong with her that she couldn't quite seem to pull it off? She ached. What was it, self-pity or justifiable mourning? A little of both, she supposed. It was going to take a while to get over this. But she would do it. She always did do what she set her mind to.

But that would come a little later. She needed some time to get herself together. She'd escaped from the horrible agony of the wedding that wasn't meant to be. And now, here she was, all alone and— She raised her head, startled. Where the hell was she, anyway?

Wait. It was coming back to her. The long, low sports car. The tall, hard and handsome man. The run on the beach. The champagne.

"Oh, my God," she moaned, lying back. Hand to her head, she tried to hold back the throbbing. She remembered it all. Well, at least she remembered most of it up to the lobster dinner. Things got a little blurry after that. But she did remember bits and pieces.

She remembered a man's arms around her, warm lips against her neck, chest hair—

"Oh, no," she groaned, squinting against the pain in her head, trying to remember more. She couldn't have...could she?

Throwing back the covers, she looked to see what she still had on. A bra and panties. Well, that was encouraging. Maybe things hadn't gone too far after all.

She stopped, thinking as hard as her headache would let her. Rafe. That was his name—or at least, the first half of it. But for some reason, she had never found out who he really was, why he was coming to her wedding, where he knew Darren from.

He'd been so, well, nice. Comforting, in a way. Unsettling in another. And though he had been there

to help her and to get her a room and to make sure she
made it through the night, he hadn't been very sym-
pathetic, as she remembered it. In fact, he'd been sort
of cold and unfeeling about a lot of things. Why? Why
had he come to the chapel? And why had he so readily
joined in on her runaway?

"Just who was that masked man?" she murmured
as she swung her legs around to get out of bed. "Do
you suppose he left a silver bullet around here some-
place?" Her head felt as big as a balloon in the Macy's
parade. The real question was now, of course, *where*
was that masked man?

He didn't seem to be here. There was no sense of a
man lurking in the closet or about to arrive, humming, from the shower. Still, he must have been here
once. How else had she ended up half-undressed?

Her gaze fell upon the objects on the table and she
walked over, stepping carefully, trying not to jolt her
head in any way. Money. And a note that said there
was a car waiting for her downstairs.

Well, that was very nice of him. Wasn't it? There
was something still nagging at the back of her con-
sciousness. Why was he doing all this? She was nothing to him.

Pictures flashed into her mind: his blue eyes; the feel
of his breath against her skin; his hand on her arm; his
tongue....

She closed her eyes and covered her ears. No! She
wouldn't think about that. She'd been weak, drunk,
in agony. Whatever had happened—and she was
pretty sure it hadn't been too extreme—she wasn't
going to dwell on it and feel guilty about it now. She
was just going to assure herself that it wouldn't hap-

pen again. She turned back to the concerns of the day and buried last night in the past.

A long, hot shower helped a lot. She came out toweling her hair, and tried to set her day in order. For right now, the question was, what on earth was she going to wear? Her wedding gown lay in a heap on the floor, and there on the chair was that awful red thing Rafe had bought her the night before. She smiled as she remembered how surprised he had looked when she'd explained to him why she had reservations about the dress. But her smile faded when she realized she was going to have to wear that outlandish costume to go down to get the car. She had nothing else.

There was money on the table. She could go downstairs and buy a summer shift or something. But she didn't want to spend the time. She wanted to get home, check her answering machine, call her mother. And she would certainly have to get hold of that Rafe person and thank him. Despite her doubts about how the evening had ended, he had been her Prince Charming in her time of need.

Moving back toward the bed, she stumbled over something. Bending down painfully, she held her breath and picked up a man's wallet. It fell open, revealing Rafe's picture on a driver's license. "Ooops," she said. "Lost your wallet, mister."

That was rather convenient, actually. It would give her an excuse to look him up. And it should contain addresses that might be helpful. She flipped through it briefly. Credit cards, business cards, a few receipts, lots of money.

"You should be more careful, Rafe," she murmured, looking back at the driver's license, curious about his last name. But the name she read couldn't be right. She read it again, and it still didn't jibe with her reality. A third time and she finally began to put two and two together and come up with a number she didn't like at all.

Raphael Tennyson.

She knew that name. Rafe was Darren's brother.

Darren's brother. Shock waves raced through her system. *Darren's brother.* Of course. No wonder he had been at the chapel. He was Darren's brother.

Darren had never tried to get her to meet his brother, but he had mentioned him a few times. She had felt Darren was pretty much in awe of his older sibling. Darren hadn't yet settled on a career, while his brother was the head of some huge corporation. And while Darren claimed to enjoy his carefree way of life, Kendall could tell the difference made him feel somewhat less than adequate. When Darren mentioned Rafe, it was usually in the form of a boast of some sort, as in, "You think he's got a great house, you should see my brother's place in San Marino."

Raphael Tennyson. Yup, that was Darren's brother, all right. And he probably knew where the skunk was hiding right now.

It made her blood boil to think of the way she had trusted him. She'd poured her heart out, cried on his shoulder, gotten drunk— Good Lord, she had let everything go in front of him, not knowing who he really was. What was he doing now, reporting to Darren on how she'd taken the news? What a rat!

She'd even— She cringed to think of it. She'd even kissed him.

Her fingers closed on the wallet, and her dark eyes took on a crafty look. Yes, what a rat. The man would definitely have to pay.

"Call for you on line two, Mr. Tennyson."

"Mr. Tennyson, Mr. Wilson would like to see you at your convenience...."

"Mr. Tennyson, the board requests..."

"Mr. Tennyson..."

"Mr. Tennyson..."

Coming in through the front lobby with its high, glass windows and modern marble sculptures, Rafe charged through the claims on his attention like a bull down a dusty Pamplona street. His suit was rumpled. His eyes were red from lack of sleep, and his face was cold as ice.

"Uh-oh," said the blonde in the typing pool to the woman who ran the copying machine. "Mr. T. is in a real mood today."

Grace Champion, Mr. Tennyson's secretary, leaned behind the watercooler and whispered to her group of confidantes, "The lion's got a thorn in his paw. Do I have a volunteer to pull it out?"

She didn't get any takers.

"Cancel all my appointments for the next hour, Grace," Rafe barked as she walked into his oak-paneled office. "We're going to be making a few phone calls."

Grace, a tall, slender African-American with the elegance and sense of style of a Parisian high-fashion model was always efficient, always ready to serve. "Phone calls, Mr. Tennyson?"

"Yes." He ran a hand through his hair and frowned. "Who do we know in Australia?"

One and a half hours of fruitless phone calls later, with a board impatiently waiting in the conference room for him to chair a meeting he'd called, Rafe had to face it. Darren hadn't gone to Australia after all. Nobody knew where Darren was. Darren just might be unfindable.

In the meantime, he couldn't get the picture of Kendall out of his mind. Kendall, alone and husbandless and pregnant. Kendall, slim and scared in the hotel room where he'd left her, huddled in a small corner of the bed. Kendall, in that damn ivory-lace bra and that tiny scrap of nylon masquerading as panties....

There it was again, that drop-away feeling in his stomach, that tightening, that clutch. He had to stop thinking about her. He had to get his mind on other things.

Glancing at his desk, his gaze lingered only briefly on the papers awaiting his signature, then went instead to two pictures, the only photographs of family he had in his office. The first was of a sweet little blonde with a winsome smile and rosy cheeks. The second was of a younger girl, darker, less happy, with secrets hidden behind eyes as black as coal. Cami and Tori were six and four years old, respectively. His daughters. Little strangers living in his house.

More problems. His life had suddenly become filled with problems. But if he could just find Darren, he might at least be able to solve the Kendall situation.

"Mr. Tennyson, the board is waiting." Grace stood her ground, but she was prepared to be growled at, and she wasn't disappointed.

"Yes, I know," Rafe said roughly, glaring at her. "I'll be in there in a moment. Tell them to play tick-tacktoe until I can make it."

"Mrs. McReady is getting especially restive. She said to tell you she has only so much time to spend on your air-headed chitchat, so make it snappy."

Mrs. McReady had been his great-grandmother's best friend. She had lived longer than anyone else and knew more about the business than anyone. Her tongue was sharp, but so was her mind. Ordinarily, she was one of his favorite people. But today, he had no patience for anyone.

Turning like a wounded bear, he barked out, "You can tell Mrs. McReady she can—"

"Wait with the rest of the board," Grace finished for him quickly. "Yes, sir, I'll do just that."

"Don't finish my sentences for me, damn it."

The vehemence of his response caught Grace by surprise, but she wouldn't give him the satisfaction of seeing her wilt. Head held high, she nodded and left the room. Rafe grimaced, wishing he had better control of his temper today. But that didn't seem possible at the moment.

What a night. What a pair of nights. He'd stopped a wedding, ruined a couple of lives, entangled himself in relationships—something he had always vowed he would never do. He hadn't gotten any work done in two days. Somewhere between Marina del Rey and home, he had lost his wallet. He hadn't had more than four hours' sleep in the last forty-eight hours. And he wasn't sure he could look forward to better conditions tonight if he didn't find Darren. He had to do something about Kendall before he could rest.

Half an hour later, Grace looked up from typing a memo to see a curious sight coming toward the office. A young woman with too much makeup and wearing white satin pumps and a tight, sleazy dress that was more appropriate for the Sunset Strip than for business stopped before her desk and smiled.

"Mr. Tennyson?" she asked.

"Mr. Tennyson is in a meeting right now. Do you have an appointment?"

The woman pouted. "Rafe's busy?"

Grace's imagination began to work overtime. This promised to be a story she was going to want to be in on. Mr. T.'s private life was off-limits to the staff. Theories about the man ran rampant, but he was very circumspect—something to do with the custody of his children or something. This lovely young woman might just be a window into that private world. She couldn't pass up the chance.

"Yes, he's meeting with the board of directors. If you would care to have a seat, perhaps I could squeeze you in before lunch...."

"I don't have time." The young woman turned, eyes narrowing, and she looked at the double doors of the conference room. "Is that where they're meeting?" she asked.

It didn't take a genius to foresee what was coming next, and Grace was a bright woman. She sprang up from behind her desk. "Oh, no, you can't go in there," she cried.

"Oh, yeah?" Kendall gave her a big smile. "Watch me."

Grace was fast on her feet, but the woman was faster. She shoved open the doors with a flourish and strode into the room with all the confidence of a conquering gladiator. She looked the room over, nodding to Rafe.

"Kendall," he breathed, his arm suspended in midair just as his thoughts were suspended in midsentence.

She smiled. "In the flesh, so to speak." She posed, letting the dress do its work on her audience. The four men on the board gaped in guilty appreciation, while the two women frowned with disapproval. Just what she'd hoped for. She grinned at Rafe, enjoying any discomfort he might already be feeling, anticipating more.

"Uh, Kendall..." Rafe had no idea what could possibly be going on here. The last time he had seen Kendall, she'd been sound asleep, her face blessed with the heavenly innocence of a child. Now she looked like... well, sin. Lots of sin, in a very attractive package. And she seemed to have something on her mind, something that required a glare at him between each phony smile.

He looked questioningly at Grace, who shrugged. She had no more idea than he did on what to do with the woman.

But Kendall didn't need anyone to help her out. She could do just fine on her own. Leaning forward, she shook hands with each of the board members close enough to reach.

"Hi, everybody. I'm Kendall McCormick. I know you all are busy. I only want a moment of your time to settle a little unfinished business of my own with this man, if you don't mind."

She leaned closer, speaking more softly, as though she were letting them all in on a great big secret.

"It's of a personal nature, but I know you all are good friends of Rafe's, so I'm sure he won't mind if I just go ahead right here and now. Right, Rafe?"

Rafe was beginning to get a very bad feeling about this, but there didn't seem much he could do to stop it, short of calling for the security guards or throwing her over his shoulder, as he had the night before. Neither option seemed to fit the moment, so he decided to wait it out. But he was beginning to understand how a man might feel in a barrel about to go over Niagara Falls—very, very nervous.

"What is it, Kendall?" he asked carefully, his face set in the hard look that usually had typists scurrying for cover and administrative assistants updating their résumés. "What can I do for you?"

She smiled, but he didn't trust it. There was something missing in that look, something that had been there quite naturally the night before. And now it was gone. Something was wrong.

"Honey," she said, her smile getting more and more brittle. "You left your wallet in the hotel room. It was right there, under the bed. It must have dropped out when... Well, you know." She smirked. "I just thought you might be needing it." Throwing him a quick, defiant glance, she slapped the thing down on the table.

Rafe nodded slowly. It was good to know where his wallet was. And she had looked at it, of course. She must have in order to have known where to find him. And that meant she knew he was Darren's brother. Hardly an earthshaking discovery. It had probably been a surprise, but so what? He couldn't quite figure out what her problem was.

"Thanks," he said, but she wasn't finished.

"And as for this money you left me..." She reached into her cleavage and pulled the stack of bills out, holding them up for all to see, then tossed them into the air. They fluttered to the table like big, green confetti. "He's a generous guy," she told the others, nodding as though they were all in on it.

The members of the board looked from her to Rafe to the money, mouths agape, but nobody said a word.

"Honey," Kendall said, addressing Rafe again, with saccharine sweetness. "You should know you don't have to pay me for what we did last night. Why, you're so good, I should be paying you." She turned conspiratorially to the others, her eyes huge. "You wouldn't believe what this man can do with a tube of toothpaste."

The gasps ringed the room, and Rafe groaned, his head falling back. "Kendall—"

Her eyes flashed, but she put on a wide, wide smile. "Don't bother seeing me out, honey. I can find my own way."

Only Rafe really understood the anger that was behind the generous smile and the compliments.

As Kendall left the room, she put on the exaggerated walk perfected by starlets in the fifties. Rafe shook his head and looked at his secretary helplessly.

Grace grinned. She'd never seen her boss stumped for words before. She kind of liked it. "Well, no one could accuse her of not knowing how to make an entrance," she said. "Or an exit, either."

Rafe opened his mouth to reply, but he never got the chance. The stunned board members had found their tongues at last, and the cries of outrage rang through the room. "Is this or is this not a place of business where professionals expect..."

"Really, Raphael, the women you cavort with..."

"Toothpaste? What did she mean by that?"

"What is this, Raphael? Are you going to prostitutes now? Your father must be turning in his grave—and your mother...! Well, I hate to think what your mother would say if she—"

Suddenly, Mrs. McReady's voice chimed in, drowning out all the others. "Oh, shut up you old fools. That girl was no prostitute." She banged her cane against the table. "Don't you know anything? She was a lovely young woman with a lot of guts." Turning to Rafe, Mrs. McReady shook her finger at him. "I say you'd better go after her, you young idiot. You've been much too stuffy much too long. A woman like that could put some color in your cheeks."

Rafe looked back at them all blankly. He hardly heard a word they'd said. There was no doubt that Kendall was angry with him. The thing was, would he ever know why? In his experience, women got angry about the strangest things. There was no telling what might have set her off. He supposed there was only one thing he could do. He was going to have to find out where she was and talk to her about it.

He sighed. He'd wanted to stay away from her until he could get Darren back to marry her. But there was no help for it. He was just going to have to do this.

Adjourning the meeting without a second thought, he wandered back into his office.

"Grace, I want you to make a call for me. Kendall McCormick runs a swim school. I want you to find out where it is."

Grace held back her grin with admirable restraint. "Yes, Mr. Tennyson. Right away, sir."

Kendall breathed in the chlorine-scented air and smiled. Children's voices echoed from wall to wall in the enclosed pool area. Water splashed. The pump droned. Home sweet home.

She was in her element here. She really ought to stick to what she knew. She was where she was happy. Out in the big, bad world, she was just a fish out of water.

"Well, I certainly learned my lesson," she said as she wrapped the old worn towel around her hips, covering the electric blue Lycra suit from the waist down.

Kim, her office manager and bookkeeper, as well as her best friend, raised her pretty face from her books and cried, "Oh, Kendall, don't say that."

Kendall picked up a stack of kick boards and shook her head. "From now on, it's going to be work, work, work. No more playing around with the fun guys."

"Oh, I could just kill Darren." Kim slammed her pencil down on the open ledger. "It's awful what he did." Her voice changed. "But listen, you need to get away, Kendall. You should take this time and go off somewhere...."

"No." Kendall shook her head. "I allotted myself one long evening of self-pity, and that's all I get." She filed away some papers, then turned back to Kim. "Self-pity is like a drug, you know. You can get addicted. If I went off to lick my wounds, I would just go over everything again and again, and there's no point to it. Life goes on. And the only way I'll have a life is if I get on with it. Nobody else is going to do it for me."

Kim sighed. "I guess you're right." Her plump face brightened. "But, hey, if you're really ready to jump back into the fray, I know this really nice man. He's a lawyer, and his wife just recently passed away."

"No. No, no, no." Kendall backed away as she spoke, shaking her head. "I'm a swim instructor. I run a swimming school. I coach a swim team. That's it. I'm not even going to be a woman anymore. I'm like this neutral being, committed to work and friendship, and that's all. Forget about men for me. I don't want them in my life."

Kim sighed as she watched her friend and employer hurry back into the pool enclosure. Poor Kendall. Some women seemed to be unlucky in love. It was going to take a good long while before she would be ready to try again, Kim thought.

It was almost two hours later when the tall, handsome man came into the office. When Kim looked up, her first thought was that he must be coming in to register his children for swimming lessons. She smiled. "May I help you?"

Blue eyes seemed to pierce right through her, taking in every detail, setting her back on her heels. "I'm looking for Kendall McCormick," the man said in a deep, masculine voice that could probably knock birds out of trees.

Kim swallowed hard and found herself stammering in a very uncharacteristic way. "S-she, uh, she's busy right now. She's teaching a class."

He cocked an eyebrow and smiled, looking like a man who knew a pretty woman when he saw one. "May I go in and watch?"

"Oh." Kim giggled, feeling pleased, feeling complimented, feeling ridiculous—and loving it. "Sure. Here, I'll show you the way."

She jumped down off her stool and led him into the pool area, a matter of a dozen feet and one doorway, a trail that surely didn't need to be blazed by a guide. But there was something about the man that made her 666want to help him. She had to restrain herself from asking if he cared to share the cranberry-juice cocktail she was saving for her lunch.

"There she is," Kim said helpfully, pointing out what was only obvious. "You can sit here in the bleachers and wait, if you want. She should be through in about ten minutes."

The man thanked her and she left regretfully, looking back three times before she disappeared back into the office.

Rafe's attention was fixed on Kendall.

She was in the water with them, her hair tied back in a thick braid that fell below her waist, the end dipping into the water like the tip of a paintbrush into paint. Six young children clustered around her, hanging on her every word, their eyes wide, their mouths open. She had them doing a breathing exercise that she demonstrated by puffing out her cheeks, chipmunk-style. The children laughed. Rafe grinned. She was good with kids, that much was obvious.

He liked watching her. She moved like a mermaid in the water, as though she'd been made for the stuff. There was something about the shape of her arm, the angle of her long neck, that sent shivers down his spine. And when she turned and saw him, her gaze hit him with an almost physical force.

She didn't smile or acknowledge him in any way. He nodded, but she didn't respond. As she turned back to the children, he frowned. She didn't look right. There was a haunted look to her eyes that he wanted to erase, wipe out, but the only way he could think of to do that was to grab her and kiss her senseless. And something told him that wouldn't be a welcome move on his part.

He had to remind himself that he had no right to touch her. In fact, he had no rights here at all. What he had was responsibility, thanks to brother Darren. Lots of lovely responsibility.

He watched her, torn by conflicting emotions. He was going to have to keep an eye on her in order to make sure she was all right. But whenever he saw her, the old juices started to flow. Could he stay close and not touch her?

He would do it. He had to do it.

Finally the lesson was over and the children headed for the locker rooms. Kendall pulled herself out of the pool, her long legs shimmering with water. She pulled a towel around her waist before walking slowly toward where he was sitting.

Her skin was clean and glowing. She looked smooth and strong, the picture of health and athleticism.

Funny, he thought, she seemed more beautiful every time he saw her.

She stopped in front of him, a step down on the bleachers so that her gaze was just about level with his. "What are you doing here?" she demanded, her eyes cool and assessing.

He wanted to smile, she looked so good, and though he kept his mouth under control, his eyes gave him away. "Watching you."

Kendall moved back a step. She wanted barriers, not bridges. "I gave you back your wallet. What more do you want?"

He shrugged nonchalantly. "World peace. My own professional football team."

"You," he could have added, but he restrained himself.

Still, she thought she read the word in the way his eyes seemed to burn as he looked at her, and suddenly, she was blushing.

Blushing. Incredible. It took her breath away. She hadn't blushed in years. Hoping he wouldn't notice, she bent to pick up a kick board left behind by one of the children. "I don't have any of those things to give you," she said quickly, turning to toss the board toward a pile of others. "So you might as well move on to greener pastures."

"How are you, Kendall?" Rafe said, holding his ground.

"Me?" She looked back at him, surprised that he'd asked. "I'm fine. Don't I look fine?"

"Oh, yes," he said softly. "You look quite fine."

She was going to blush again if she didn't watch out. To give herself something to do, she came up another step and swung onto the seat beside him.

"So, you and Darren are really brothers," she said, looking at him.

"Yes. We're really brothers." He moved uncomfortably. "But I didn't come to talk to you about that."

She was staring, searching for something she wasn't detecting. "You know, I'm finding it very hard to believe," she said, scrutinizing him carefully. There wasn't a thing about him that reminded her of her ex-fiancé. "You don't look alike. Or act alike, actually."

"We have different mothers," Rafe said shortly. The smile had vanished from his eyes. It was evident he didn't much like the turn the conversation was taking. Still, he went on and explained. "My mother was the original, my father's high school sweetheart who worked to put him through grad school. The one he divorced to make way for Darren's mother."

"The younger woman," Kendall guessed, reading the bitterness in his eyes.

"Of course."

That might account for the difference in their personalities as well as their looks. It also made for some intriguing speculations, things that she would dearly love to get into. But getting into them would mean getting closer to Rafe. And getting close to this man was not something she could risk at the present time.

Her new resolution was to steer clear of all men, and it looked relatively easy to do in theory. Most of the men she knew would be simple to reject. Even Darren, should he come back. But there was something about Rafe, something about his hard blue eyes and strong, sensual face that made her determination falter. She'd kissed this man yesterday, and she remembered it. It was pretty obvious he remembered it, too.

She was going to have to harden herself against him. Talking about his problems wasn't going to help her do that. She frowned, giving herself a mental pep talk.

This man is poison, Kendall. Stay tough.

"Why are you so angry with me?" he asked, as though he could read the workings of her mind.

She hesitated. Maybe he wasn't so all-knowing after all. How could he not understand that? "You didn't tell me who you were. You let me think you were just anybody, somebody I could lean on, confide in, depend on. And all the time, you were Darren's brother."

"Would knowing I was his brother have made a difference?"

Her chin rose. "Sure. I could have started hating you that much sooner."

His laugh was short and heartfelt. "You can't hate me because of my brother," he told her with a grin. "It's against the rules. You can be angry, though. And I guess you are."

"You could say I was angry at you, I suppose..." she said slowly, deciding to level with him. "But the truth is, mostly I'm angry at you because Darren's not around to be angry at."

He nodded. He could accept that.

"But..." She flashed a look at him out of the corners of her eyes and went on. "I am sorry about that little scene in your office yesterday. Revenge may be sweet, but it's also rather childish."

"I don't get stunned easily." He turned to look at her. "But you did a job on me. I was speechless." He shook his head, amusement flickering in his eyes. "I still feel like it must have been a dream."

She couldn't repress her grin. "It was pretty funny, though, wasn't it? The looks on their faces."

Without meaning to, Rafe found himself grinning right back at her. "You've destroyed my reputation."

"No kidding? Good. They seemed like sort of a stuffy bunch. I hope they were really outraged." A thought occurred to her, and she turned toward him anxiously. "You won't lose your job or anything, will you?"

He wanted to wrap his arms around her and hold her close. She wasn't nearly as tough as she wanted to be. "No, Kendall. I'm pretty much the boss. They couldn't get rid of me if they wanted to."

"Oh." Now she was embarrassed that she'd shown concern. "Well, good. I guess." Her eyes met his, and she knew if she didn't look away quickly, they would start smiling at each other again and things would go from bad to worse very rapidly. She quickly gave him some information guaranteed to put them back on a distrustful basis. "There was a message from your darling brother on my answering machine when I got home."

Rafe stiffened, looking at her sharply. "What did he say?"

"Let's see if I can quote it.... He said, 'Hi babe. Sorry I couldn't hack the wedding thing. I gave it a run, but the wave died out on me. I gotta get out of town, get my head together, you know? I'll give you a call when I get back. Oh, by the way, if you need some

money to help pay for the wedding and all that, call
my brother, Raphael. In fact, just bill him. He'll take
care of it. Ciao, baby.' "

"He didn't say that." But Rafe knew that Darren
probably had. The words sounded so familiar. Rafe's
opinion of his brother dropped another set of notches.

"He did. I didn't erase it. You want to come over
and hear for yourself?"

No. He believed her. And that made it all the more
unbelievable that she would be in love with the jerk.

"Kendall, of course, I want to take care of Darren's debts. I'll reimburse you for whatever you had to
pay for the wedding."

The eyes she turned his way were cold and hard as
stone. "You can keep your money, Mr. Tennyson. I
don't want it. And neither do my parents." She stood
up to leave. "I have another lesson in fifteen minutes."

Looking across the pool, he could see the children
and a few parents beginning to gather. "Have dinner
with me tonight," he said without looking back at her.

"What? Are you crazy?"

Rafe looked up at her then, his blue eyes staring
right into hers. Yes, he supposed he was. He needed
to stay away from her. He should make all contact by
phone. If he saw her again, if he took her to dinner, if
they were alone together . . . He knew what was going
to happen. And so did she.

But he was crazy. He couldn't stop. "Please. I'd
appreciate it if you would. We need to talk."

Her heart was beating faster and Kendall knew she
had to avoid seeing him again at all costs. "We have
talked. I think we must have covered everything by

now." She began to make her way down out of the bleachers.

He watched her for a moment, then rose and followed her. "Kendall, wait." He stopped her with a hand on her arm. She turned and looked up at him, waiting, and there it was again, that haunted look he hated. His fingers tightened on her flesh. "If I got him back here, would you marry him?" Rafe asked harshly, not sure he really wanted an answer, but knowing he had to ask the question.

Her eyes mirrored her shock. "What?"

"Would you give him another chance?"

Her breath was suddenly coming very fast, and she couldn't quite catch the rhythm again. "Rafe, what are you talking about?"

He could see that she was agitated, but it was hard to tell if it was because of love or anger. Did she want Darren back? And if she did, could she admit it even to herself?

"I'm looking for him," Rafe said slowly, watching her eyes. "I've hired a private investigator."

"A private investigator?" She put her hand over her heart and took a deep breath, trying to steady herself.

"Yes." He was still holding her arm. "And when I get him back here, I'm going to put the two of you together in a room and..."

"No!" She pulled out of his grasp and began to back away from him, her eyes full of dread. "No, under no circumstances do I ever want to see Darren Tennyson again."

Rafe moved forward, not letting her get away. "But do you still love him?" he insisted, wanting to know, needing to know.

"Love? Hah." She swung around, her mood completely changed. She was no longer frightened, but angry, and it felt so much more comfortable. "Don't talk to me about love. It's a phony concept. Have you ever actually loved anyone?"

"Kendall, calm down." Rafe frowned, surprised by her vehemence. "I don't need a lecture on love."

Her eyes flashed. "I beg to differ." That was obviously exactly what he needed. "Do you know what love is? Can you put love in a petri dish and analyze it? Can you put it up on a screen and study it?"

He stared at her, fascinated. Hadn't he made this very argument himself at some time in the past? He seemed to remember a country lane, a lovely blonde in the front seat of his silver-blue Mercedes. She had been holding out for love, he had been denying its existence. At the time his position had seemed brilliant strategy. Now, the same opinions being spouted by Kendall seemed silly rationalizations.

"Love is a lot like self-pity," she lectured sternly. "It does nothing but weaken you."

"Forget about love," he said evenly. "Pretend I never brought it up."

But Kendall had been saying these things in her head all day and she was glad for the opportunity to share them with civilization at large. "Are you in love with anyone?" she demanded.

Rafe sighed, giving up. It might be best to let her get these things out of her system. "No."

"Have you ever been?"

His eyes darkened. He wished they could do this without getting into his personal life. "I thought I was once upon a time," he admitted reluctantly.

She nodded, sure she was on the right track. "What happened?"

His eyes were hooded, and his face was hard again. "Things...didn't work out."

She nodded as though she'd known it all along. "So...what is your conclusion? Did love die? Or did it turn out that love was just some sort of mirage that didn't mean anything anyway?" It was pretty obvious what her ruling was, and since she was in charge of this lecture, it seemed a done deal.

Meanwhile, the kids were gathering for their lesson and the parents were beginning to look across the pool with more than a little curiosity. Kendall seemed to have forgotten all about them, but Rafe hadn't, and they were beginning to make him a bit uncomfortable.

He glanced back at her, almost angry. "Kendall, I'm not going to stand here on the side of a pool explaining what happened to my marriage."

She'd gone too far and she realized it. "No, of course, you're not. I'm sorry." She brightened. "But we're talking theory and generalities, anyway. I'm not asking you to reveal secrets. We're exploring truth. And the truth is, love is just a lot of wishful thinking—projecting feelings onto other people that you wish they had."

She was incredibly bitter and cynical. It reminded Rafe a lot of the way he had felt around the time of his divorce. He hated to see her this way. She couldn't possibly have been like this before Darren had done his number on her.

Darren—hell, who was kidding whom here? Rafe had been the one who had done it to her. Darren was just a weak link in a chain. Rafe had been the one who'd picked up the clippers and cut the thing all to pieces.

He wanted to talk to her, to explain, maybe even to tell her the truth, but the crowd gathering on the other side of the pool was inhibiting him. They couldn't talk here.

Grabbing her hand, Rafe pulled Kendall into the lifeguard office, out of sight of the others. "Kendall, there are so many things I want to say to you," he said quickly, touching her hair with the flat of his hand and looking down at her fiercely. "I don't want anything to happen to you."

She searched his face. "Nothing is going to happen to me," she assured him, puzzled.

"Are you eating right? Do you drink milk?"

"What?"

"You know you have to be careful, do all the right things." He touched her cheek. "Kendall, I want to be there for you. I know it's going to be hard, especially in the coming months...."

She stared up at him, startled. What was this man's problem? He seemed overly intense. So his brother had dumped her, it wasn't his fault. He didn't have to take over where his brother had left off. She was a big girl. She could take care of herself.

"In the coming months," she cut in, "I plan to have a whole new life going for me. And, pardon me, I don't mean to be rude, but this life I plan isn't going to have a Tennyson in it."

That set him back, but only for a moment. Rafe had a sudden flash of insight and knew without a doubt that her words were mere bravado. She wasn't going to be able to hold him off forever. When she needed him, he would be there.

He was still gazing at her as though he knew something about her, was in on some secret. Kendall had about had it with his proprietary attitude—not to mention the way he disturbed her state of mind. She turned and started for the door, but now that he had her blood pounding in annoyance, she remembered that she had another bone to pick with him. Stopping, she turned and looked back defiantly.

"And by the way, I don't know what all we did the other night...."

His head went back and his eyes looked deep as the ocean. "You mean, you don't remember?"

She licked her dry lips and shifted her gaze. "Not... not everything."

He couldn't help it. He had to taunt her a little. "You mean you don't really remember how good I was?"

She paled visibly, her eyes widening. "We didn't—"

"Make love?" The words seemed to stick in his throat, and suddenly the whole thing didn't seem so funny any longer. "Don't worry, Kendall. You fought hard, but I held you off."

She drew in a sharp breath and stared at him, but in the end, she didn't believe him. Without another word, she whirled and left him behind.

Kendall threw herself into her work with such a vengeance she didn't even see when Rafe finally left the pool area. Memories of him and the night in the hotel kept trying to intrude on her concentration, but she wasn't going to let that happen. She was no young girl. She understood what worked and what didn't. She had her plans, and they didn't include him.

But just what was she going to do with her life? That was the question that kept nipping at her throughout the day and into the evening. Not get married, that was for sure. Every relationship she'd had in the past ten years had turned out to be a dud. She was through with trying. Maybe she was just too old to adjust to a man and his ways. Maybe she was too old to really attract the right one. She wasn't sure what it was, and she didn't want to analyze it at this point. She just wanted to move on.

Her new philosophy on the actual existence of love was still shaky, but that seemed to be the way to go.

"I don't need a man in my life," she told herself. "I can be happy without that."

After all, she'd been a happy woman before she'd met Darren. She enjoyed her work and her friends. Building her business and teaching swim classes and coaching the swim team were fulfilling activities. That should be enough for her.

Anyway, just how many married women did she know who were absolutely miserable with the men they'd picked and the life they were forced to lead? She was perfectly happy with what she had. She couldn't have it all, but what she did have was pretty good. She would have her share, and that was enough.

Wasn't it?

At any rate, she was going to stay away from the Tennysons. And that was a promise.

Five

A few days later, Kendall was in the middle of making arrangements for private home swim lessons with a man sporting a heavy Southern accent when something began setting off warning signals inside her. She had the address and had agreed to show up every afternoon at three for the next two weeks, but there was something about that voice....

"Now, Mr. Smith, you say you have two little girls?"

"Yes ma'am. Cami and Tori. They're six and four years old, and neither one of them can swim a lick."

Swim a lick? Hmm. She stared at the name she had written down. Mr. John Smith. Phony-sounding name. Phony-sounding accent. Suddenly everything fell into place. Taking a deep breath, she glared at the receiver.

"Rafe Tennyson, this is you, isn't it?"

There was a pause, and then the voice came back with the accent thicker than ever. "Why ma'am, how could you suggest such a thing? I hope you realize you are on the verge of impugning the honor of a fine Southern gentleman...."

"What on earth are you thinking of? Just because I won't have dinner with you, you're going to lure me out to your house with lies about children who need swimming lessons?"

"Hey, hold on a minute. That part is true," Rafe said, his normal voice miraculously restored. "I do have two little girls, Kendall. And they do need lessons."

She stopped, exasperated. It was true she had been avoiding him, but he knew as well as she did that staying away from each other was the only way to deal with the strange attraction they seemed to have between them. Why couldn't he just forget she existed? They'd almost become relatives, but that had fallen through, so there was really no reason to keep up this connection. Why couldn't he accept that?

"There are other swim instructors," she told him. "I think you'd better call one of them."

"I want you, Kendall. I watched you with those kids at the pool. You'd be perfect. You see—" his tone took on a sudden depth of sincerity that made her listen a little more closely "—their mother died a few months ago. They've just come to live with me. I've got this huge pool in the backyard and I don't think either one of them is water safe. Seriously, Kendall, I'm worried about their safety, and I know you're the one to take care of this."

She rolled her eyes. For all she knew, he was handing her a complete line of bull. She knew he was divorced. She hadn't known about the children. But at his age, a couple of kids would seem pretty normal. And she supposed it could be that his ex-wife had died, leaving him with two little girls to raise on his own. So maybe he was telling the truth. And if he was, the thought of those two little girls living with this rough, arrogant man did tug at her a bit.

"You really do have two kids?" she asked, just to make sure.

"I really do. Will you do it?"

She sighed. "Tell you what. I'll come out Monday and give them a trial lesson and we'll see how things look. Okay?"

"That would be great. Thanks, Kendall."

She hated that smug male sound in his voice, but what could she do? He thought he had manipulated her, and he was right; he had.

A sudden thought came to her and she stopped him before he got away. "Rafe, I'm warning you, if this has anything to do with trying to get me back with Darren..."

"Oh, no, don't worry," he said quickly. "I haven't seen or heard from Darren since—"

"Since the wedding that never was? Good. Because, Rafe, if I see any sign that Darren has even been there, I'll turn around and leave so fast, you'll be dizzy."

"I understand..." He hesitated. "Listen, Kendall, the Southern accent was just a joke, really. I thought you'd see through it even sooner than you did. I'm not out to trick you. Not in any way. I just want to make sure you understand that."

"I understand it, Rafe. Whether or not I believe it is another matter entirely."

For the rest of the day, Kendall could hardly keep her mind on her lessons. So, Rafe had two little girls. What was he like with children? She couldn't imagine. Did the children look like him? Were they over their mother's death? Kendall didn't know why these questions wouldn't leave her alone, but they clung, popping up at the most awkward moments.

What was Rafe to her, anyway?

"Nothing," she said aloud, slamming her fist into a towel. "Not a damn thing." But that was a lie and she knew it, even as the words were leaving her lips.

Rafe had some sort of hold on her and it was more than just the fact that he was Darren's brother. He loomed large to her. He had put himself in her life and no matter how much she protested, something told her he was there to stay for a while. She might as well get used to it and meet him head-on rather than try to hide from him all the time.

Monday came quickly. Kendall noticed that her car seemed to be going slower and slower as she neared the address Rafe had given her. There was no use trying to deny she was nervous about seeing him again. The trouble was, she was never her normal self around him. Somehow, he always managed to throw her off, make her feel as though she were forging into uncharted territory with him.

Okay—the truth. He scared her.

His house was at the end of a cul-de-sac. A long driveway led up the hill to a beautiful, split-level, ranch-style home surrounded by stately oaks. She didn't know how many acres of property he had, but the impression was of a small estate surrounded by woods.

"Quite striking," she murmured to herself, sitting at the bottom of the drive and looking up. He was already starting to intimidate her, and she hadn't even seen him yet.

She had just about finished convincing herself to begin making her way up the hill when something bright and quick caught her eye. She turned just in time to catch a glimpse of a little blond girl before she disappeared behind a large bush.

Very curious. There was no doubt in her mind that the little girl was hiding. Pretending not to have noticed a thing, Kendall pulled the car slowly up the drive and drew to a stop only when she was beyond the curve from the street. Moving as quietly as she could, she got out of the car and walked back along the drive, straining to see who was hiding among the trees and bushes at the entry gate.

There were two little girls, not just one, each with a backpack strapped to her back. They whispered to each other and looked out toward the street as though planning strategy.

"Need a ride, girls?" Kendall asked.

They both jumped a foot into the air, screamed and clung to each other in terror.

Kendall smiled at them, holding up a hand to quiet their yelling. "Hey, it's all right. I'm a friend. Are you two Cami and Tori?"

They nodded, staring at her with wide eyes.

"Good. I'm Kendall McCormick. You can call me Kendall. I came to give you swimming lessons, so why are you skipping out on me?"

Still speechless, the girls merely stared.

"Hey, cute backpacks," Kendall said, coming closer. "What have you got in there?"

The girls exchanged a worried glance, then the blonde, the older of the two, looked up and spoke hoarsely. "Our clothes." Her eyes were wide and honest. "And some cookies."

"Oh." Kendall nodded, forcing back the smile that threatened. "Running away from home?"

They looked at her with dread and nodded, obviously not yet skilled in covering their tracks.

Kendall bit her lip and pretended to think hard for a moment. "Well, you know, since I've come all this way to give you lessons, why don't we do that first? You could always run away later. What do you say?"

The older girl looked at her sister, then came closer to where Kendall was standing. "We don't want swimming lessons," she explained in a loud whisper. "Tori's afraid you'll make her go in the deep end. She's scared of the deep end."

The darker, younger girl stared at Kendall with quiet intensity, her eyes worried, her little body tense. Kendall could feel the prickly barriers she'd built up around her. Tori was not going to be easy to befriend, but Kendall had worked with tough cases before. She smiled at the girl.

"Tori is going to stay on the steps today," Kendall proclaimed as though it were the most natural thing in the world. "Unless she asks for permission to go out farther."

"Honest?" Cami looked at Tori and nodded encouragement. "Did you hear what she said?"

Tori's dark head bobbed up and down, but the little girl still didn't smile.

"Come on," Kendall said, holding out her hands to the two of them. "Let's get going. I can hardly wait to see your pool."

They came along as though they knew her well, skipping to keep up with her longer stride.

"We have a slide," Cami told her. "And a whirlpool."

"Lucky," Kendall said. "I don't have either one of those things at my pool."

She let them both into the car, where they sat side by side in the back seat. Before closing the door, Kendall leaned in and smiled at them. "Was that why you two were running away? Because Tori is afraid of the deep end?"

Cami shook her head. "Uh-uh."

She looked at them for a long moment while they stared right back at her. "Are you going to give me a hint?" she asked at last, smiling.

Cami looked at Tori and seemed to get agreement, although Kendall couldn't have pinpointed just how Tori communicated it with that small, dark, stony face.

"It's our daddy," Cami said softly. "We don't like him."

Kendall felt the air go out of her as though she'd just been hit in the stomach. This was Rafe they were talking about. He might be annoying, he was certainly overbearing, but surely he didn't deserve this. Her heart broke for him, and at the same time, fury filled her. What on earth had this man been doing to turn these children against him?

Somehow, she kept the smile on her face as she turned and closed the car door, then walked around the car and got into the driver's seat. At the same time, she was calming herself. They were just kids, after all. Kids got upset over the smallest things. Surely when she got to the bottom of this, she would find out it was something as simple as, as . . .

"Why don't you like him?" she asked as she started the car up the hill.

"He's mean," Cami said, leaning forward. Now that she'd begun, she seemed eager to list her grievances. "He always yells at us to be quiet. Tori doesn't want to go to bed when it's still light outside, and he makes us. Tori wants to camp out in a tent, but he won't let us. And when Mrs. McReady said we could have one of her kittens, he said no. So Tori said we should run away."

Kendall glanced back at Tori's silent face, which was registering no dissent at all to the catalogue of Rafe's sins. They were such beautiful children, dressed so nicely in expensive clothes, probably purchased at the very best children's boutiques, living in a gorgeous home in an exclusive neighborhood, and their complaints were identical to any other kid's anywhere in town. Only there was an extra ingredient here. Obviously, they didn't really know their father.

"Where were you going to run to?" she asked casually.

There was nothing but silence in answer, and Kendall wished she hadn't asked. Probably they had no idea. After all, the one person who had kept them safe and loved all their short lives was gone to a place they could never find, no matter how hard they ran. How completely devastating it must be to lose your mother at such a young and vulnerable age.

All the more reason their father had to be a refuge for them. She was going to have to talk to Rafe to see just exactly what was going on. It could be that he resented having these little ones thrust upon him. After all, he wasn't the sort to want to bandage scraped knees and read bedtime stories. And if that was the way the land lay—well, he was going to have to mend things.

But for now, she had lessons to give. The pool was stunning, a kidney-shaped body of blue water bordered by rocks and a small waterfall meant to make it look like something found in a forest glen. The configuration didn't do much for lessons or serious lap swimming, but it certainly looked pretty.

She coaxed both of the girls into the pool, although it was immediately apparent that neither one of them was familiar with the water at all. She concentrated on getting them to lose their fear, playing games and splashing gently until they got used to the things water could do. Halfway through the hour, she looked up and saw Rafe watching them from the sun deck, which overlooked the pool, leaning on the railing, dark glasses covering his eyes. She didn't wave. She didn't want the girls to realize he was there and find their inhibitions again.

But the sight of him, so remote, so cut off from his own children and their hopes and fears, saddened her. Was this the way he wanted it? She certainly hoped not.

Rafe wasn't giving much thought to his children at that moment. As he leaned against the railing and looked down at the scene below, his mind was full of Kendall.

It had been a stroke of genius bringing her here to teach swimming, and he congratulated himself on it. Piano lessons were never like this. The view just wasn't the same. Kendall had a body that was made for the modern one-piece swimsuit. Just watching her made him breathe a little faster.

He remembered how she'd looked in the lamplight when he had undressed her, and his body tightened in agony, like that of some hormone-crazed adolescent who couldn't control himself. Damn it all, what was it with this woman? Why did she do this to him?

He'd had plenty of women in his life, beautiful women, sexy women, women who knew how to make a man feel like a king. But not one of them had taken hold of his soul the way this one had.

It had to be because he couldn't have her that he wanted her so badly. What else could it be? She was carrying his brother's child.

He was going to find Darren and bring him back and make him marry her if it was the last thing he did. And yet, the thought of Darren holding Kendall made Rafe want to go out and kill something.

Her laughter carried on the breeze, and he groaned softly. He'd been crazy to bring her here. But he had to keep an eye on her. What else could he do?

Lurching away from the railing, he went back into the house to bury himself in work, if that was at all possible.

When the lesson was over, Kendall helped the girls dry off and put on their robes. She told them silly jokes, and Cami laughed and Tori almost smiled.

"You're not going to run away now, are you?" she asked nonchalantly just before leaving them. "If you run away, we can't have our lesson tomorrow."

"Will you come every day?" Cami asked brightly.

"Every weekday," Kendall agreed, smiling. "Would you like that?"

Cami nodded. "We won't run away yet," she promised. "Maybe later."

Kendall grinned. "Okay, you two. See you tomorrow." And then it was time to beard the lion in his lair.

The maid directed her to the study where Rafe was waiting. He was working on some papers at his desk, but he looked up when the door opened. For a moment, Kendall stood in the doorway, looking at him. He didn't speak right away, but his gaze held hers and said things to her she knew he wasn't about to put into words—things she didn't want to hear.

"You came," he said at last, leaning back in his chair.

"You thought I might go back on my word?" She entered the room slowly, not wanting to get too close.

His mouth curved into a shallow smile. "Actually, I was afraid you might send a substitute."

Maybe she should have. He was not an easy man to approach. He...disturbed her—that was the word. He ruffled her feathers, and made her blood race, and made her angry and excited all at the same time. It was a purely chemical reaction, of course, just animal magnetism that meant nothing in the long run. But it threw her off stride, made her look around for things to lean on, especially when he gave her that long, dark look that belonged in a French film.

For a moment, she was tempted to turn and make a run for it. But she had to stay. She had to think of the girls, her new little charges. She had to deal with their relationship to this man. If she didn't do something, who would?

She sat down on the edge of the chair that faced the desk and forced herself to hold his gaze with her own. "Your little girls are darlings," she said. "And very teachable."

"Good."

She gave him a slight smile. "It seems odd to think of you as a father."

His blue eyes glistened like cut stones, showing no emotion. "It seems even odder to me."

"Really?" Well, that might explain part of the problem. "The girls didn't live with you when...?"

He moved impatiently. He didn't want to talk about this. Remembering his marriage was painful, especially the time of the split. For a moment, he thought of Kendall's little diatribe against the concept of love of a few days before. He'd thought he loved his wife. She'd said she loved him. When it all turned to ashes, it was as though something beloved had changed into a monster in his arms. He'd turned against her, turned against everything that had to do with her. And in the process, he'd hurt the children. That was wrong. He wished it had never happened, but he didn't have the slightest idea of how to turn it around at this point. All he could do was go on from here and do the best he could.

"Marci and I separated before Tori was born," he said shortly, reluctantly, looking away. "And I wasn't much of an absentee father to them."

Kendall stared at him, trying without success to analyze what he'd said, the way he'd said it. She couldn't tell for sure if his failure as a father was a point of pride with him or something he regretted. "So when they came to live here, you were a virtual stranger to them."

"You might say that." He turned and looked at her, his eyes strangely clouded. She was getting too close. "But what does that have to do with anything?"

He might as well have said, "This is none of your business." All she could manage was a half smile. He seemed cold today, fierce, as though he were angry about something.

That shouldn't make her nervous. She'd met his anger before and challenged it. But there was something about the room, something about seeing him here in his home that gave him the advantage. Still, she had a mission to perform. She knew he wasn't going to like this, but she had to do it.

Taking a deep breath, she went on. "It is interesting to know the background of your relationship with the girls. The fact that they hardly know you…might explain…" She steeled herself. "It might explain why they were running away from home when I arrived today."

His face closed down immediately with the hard look Kendall was beginning to recognize, the look that was meant to cover up any real emotions that might try to show themselves.

"What are you talking about?" he growled, his shoulders tensing beneath the white shirt.

"They were down near the street when I drove up, little packs on their backs, heading for the hills like escapees from a prison camp."

"What?" He grimaced. If she was telling the truth, he had to get to the bottom of this fast. He rose and started toward the door.

Kendall sprang up to stop him. This wasn't the reaction she wanted. "No, Rafe, don't go and yell at them. That's the worst thing you could do right now."

But if he didn't yell at them, how could he stop them? It was dangerous for them to go wandering down by the street. He might not understand them, but he loved them with a savage intensity he hadn't even begun to explore as yet. They were his now, and he would protect them with his life, if need be.

His eyes, when he turned to look at Kendall, were still tough, but now they had a slightly lost look. "I'm not going to yell at them," he protested, looking at her almost helplessly, angry at the feeling gnawing in him. "I just want to find out why they think they need to run away, that's all."

She breathed a sigh of relief. His icy exterior had cracks, after all. He cared about those girls. He just didn't have a clue as to how he should act around them.

"I think I can tell you why," Kendall said, wanting to be gentle but firm at the same time. She ticked off the reasons on her fingers. "You won't let them have a kitten. You won't let them camp out. You won't let them stay up until dark. You yell too much. You're mean."

"Mean . . . ?" Now he was angry enough to let it show in the steel-blue of his eyes. "Mean?"

"Rafe . . ." Kendall put a hand on his arm, feeling a mixture of empathy for his impotent pain and amusement at his frustration. It was pretty evident that he had no idea of what he was doing with these children. "Do you ever really communicate with them?"

He looked resentful of her question. "Sure I do. All the time."

"Really? We're not talking about yelling at them to be quiet, now. We're not talking about telling them to mind their manners or not to be late or to keep away from the fire. We're talking about *communication*. About finding out what they did today and how they feel about things. Do you ever do that?"

He frowned at her fiercely, disdaining to answer, but his silence on the subject was eloquent. She smiled at him, her eyes warming.

"Rafe, they're little, sad people. They've had a lot of tragedy to deal with. They need you to be strong and to give their life structure. I'm sure you do that very well. But they also need you to open up to them, to show them who you are, to let them know you care about them." Her voice softened. "To let them know they can love you if they want."

The anger had faded, but the hard look in his eyes was firmly intact. Still, she could see he had heard her.

"Do you charge extra for the lectures in child rearing?" he asked gruffly at last, glancing at her. And then, suddenly, he was looking down at her hand on his arm.

She drew it back quickly, as though she'd been burned. It was happening again, as it always did around him. Her heart was beating very fast. He was so close. He didn't have to touch her; all he had to do was look at her with that deep, penetrating darkness in his eyes and she began to throb in some sort of mystical response.

"No charge," she said breathlessly. "Consider it a bonus that comes with the basic service."

His eyes didn't change and he didn't say anything. She swallowed hard, looking at him, and then she had to turn away, groping for the door. But he reached out and caught the end of her braid in his hand, forcing her to turn back.

"How are you, Kendall?" he asked, his eyes searching hers. "Is everything all right?"

For a moment she couldn't imagine why he was asking, but then she realized he must mean emotionally because of Darren leaving her with a supposedly broken heart.

"I'm fine, Rafe. You don't have to worry about me."

"Don't I?" He wished he could believe that. But what was the point? If he weren't worrying, he would be thinking about her anyway—about her long, thick hair and the way her tongue flickered out to wet her lower lip and the way her breasts filled the top of her turquoise swimsuit with that tantalizing curve that made his fingers itch to touch her.

His hand was still in her braid, and he tugged her nearer. Her face was so close, he could smell her hair, feel the whisper of her breath against his skin. Her lips were parting. All he had to do was move two inches and he would have her under his control again. An ache ran through him, crying out for her.

She was trying hard to hide it, but it was there. He could see it shimmering in her eyes. She felt the way he did. He wanted her with a low, pulsing need that was going to drive him mad. And she wanted him, too, whether she knew it or not.

So that made them both fools. Because they couldn't have each other. Not now. Maybe not ever.

Abruptly, he released her and turned away. ''You'd better go,'' he said harshly.

She stared at him for a moment, stunned by what had almost happened, by what hadn't happened. What exactly did he want from her? She knew he was attracted, that much was all too obvious. But he kept drawing back as though there were something about her that repelled him. It was maddening.

It was also lucky. After all, she didn't want to start anything with him. She'd sworn off love altogether. Even more, she wouldn't have touched Rafe if he'd wanted her to. He was Darren's brother. There was something unnatural about turning from one brother to another just because the first one had stood you up. It was something to be avoided at all costs.

Turning away, she started to move, going toward the doorway, not thinking, just reacting to the dread.

"Will you be back tomorrow?" he asked before she had made it out the door.

She turned back to look at him. She knew she ought to run as fast as she could and never look back. But instead, she nodded. There was no point in fighting it. "Yes. I'll be back." And she made her escape through the door.

Six

The girls were waiting alongside the pool the next afternoon, the maid hovering over them to supervise, when Kendall arrived. Cami jumped up to greet her like an old friend, and Tori almost smiled.

"Today we'll start working on floating," Kendall told them as she put down her canvas bag and rummaged through it for her towel.

Cami's face went stiff. "In the deep end?" she asked anxiously. "Tori's scared of the deep end."

"Right by the stairs," Kendall assured her, tousling her hair. "I told you, you both can stay on the stairs every day until you ask me to let you out into the pool."

That seemed to satisfy them, and they went into the water gladly. But as Kendall turned to throw off her cover-up, she found them both staring at her with open mouths.

"Hey, you two. What's lesson number one?"

"Faces wet," Cami cried, obliging with a large splash.

Tori copied her sister, but a moment later, Kendall found them staring at her again, seemingly fascinated by something in the region of her belly button.

"What is it, girls? Do I have flowers growing out of my middle?"

They giggled but shook their heads and wouldn't explain. Kendall went on with the lesson, but from time to time, she caught one or the other sneaking a look at her midsection again.

She was beginning to get paranoid, glancing down all the time to see what could possibly be wrong. But there wasn't a thing. Just some crazy kick the kids were on, she decided.

"Did you talk to your daddy today?" she asked when they had finished their practice kicks.

They both turned huge eyes to stare into hers, but they didn't say a word.

"Come on, that's not such a hard question." She was curious to see if he had taken her advice. "Did your daddy sit down and talk to you this morning?"

Cami nodded. "How did you know?" she asked.

Kendall grinned, gratified. "A little bird told me." He was actually taking her advice. She felt a thrill of accomplishment. Maybe that meant he took her more seriously than she thought. "What did he talk to you about?" she asked lightly, not really wanting to pry, but wanting them to share it and get comfortable with the concept of talking to daddies.

But the reaction she received surprised her and made her wonder if she should have brought it up. Cami was looking very guilty.

"Hey, you don't have to tell me if you don't want to," she assured them cheerfully. "You and your daddy can talk about anything you want. It's none of my business."

Cami's guilty look only deepened. "He talked to us about you," she whispered at last.

Kendall was startled. "About me?" All scruples about not prying were thrown to the winds. "What about me?"

"Daddy said we should do what you say. But we really have to be careful we don't kick you or hit you or bump our head into you."

Was that all? Kendall swallowed her grin. "Well, that's very nice. Did he tell you why I deserve all this kid-glove treatment?"

Cami nodded solemnly, her blue eyes huge. "He said you had a baby in there."

Kendall blinked. Wait a minute. This wasn't right. "A baby?" she echoed faintly, looking from one to the other of them in bewilderment. "Where?"

Cami pointed. "In your tummy." She looked up into Kendall's face. "Is it a boy baby or a girl baby?"

Shock radiated through Kendall as she took in what this meant. Rafe thought she was pregnant. Rafe, the man who looked at her as though there were something burning inside him that only she could quench. He thought she was pregnant with his brother's child.

The implications of that revelation were too staggering to contemplate at the moment.

"Sorry, Cami," she said, her voice shaking a little. "Your daddy is wrong. There's no baby in there."

She went on with the lesson, but her insides were churning. Little things she'd thought were odd came back in a new light. All his protestations about her drinking the other night, his constant concern for how she was feeling, his insistence that she eat right and drink her milk—things she had taken as rather odd, but nice bits of evidence of his concern. Now she realized what it had all been about. He thought she was pregnant.

And that meant he probably thought Darren was planning to marry her because she was pregnant. And had backed out because he felt trapped.

She was mad now, boiling, raging angry. How dare he? Here, all this time she thought he was being nice, concerned about her, and the whole time, it was because he thought she was pregnant. She had a few choice words to say to him, as soon as she got the chance. Glancing at her watch every few moments, she was champing at the bit.

A car arrived as Kendall and the girls were wrapping up lessons and drying off. As the three of them watched, an elegantly dressed lady descended from a large luxury sedan and made her way to the front door.

"Ooh, it's Miss Vandergroven," Cami said, making a face. "She likes Daddy."

Kendall didn't like Daddy much herself at the moment, but she realized other women might not have her unique point of view. "Ah. And does Daddy like her?"

Cami shrugged. "I don't know. He kissed her once." She looked up from under her eyebrows. "Tori doesn't like her."

"You don't?" Kendall looked at the younger girl, but, true to form, she didn't say a thing. Still, Cami seemed to know exactly what Tori would have said if only she'd found the words.

"No, she doesn't like her." Cami shook her wet curls. "She's not very nice. She smiles at Tori and sticks her fingers in her hair like she likes her, but then if Daddy goes away, she gets mean. She smacked Tori's hand when she reached for a potato chip."

"Oh, she did, did she?" Perhaps this charming lady was the current love of Rafe's life. Kendall certainly hoped so. She stuffed her towel away in her bag as though she were wrapping it around Rafe's head. "You girls go watch a little television, why don't you. I think I'll go in and meet Miss Vandergroven."

Kendall was primed for a fight. Having an audience wasn't ideal, but getting the opportunity to do something to mess up an assignation Rafe might be having certainly was. She would definitely risk it. Leaving her cover-up behind, she went into the house in her persimmon-colored Lycra swimsuit with the deep-cut cleavage and the legs cut so high, she felt as though she were wearing a thong on a Brazilian beach. She knew her tight, well-rounded figure looked stunning in this suit, and today she was prepared to use every weapon in her arsenal.

She found Rafe and his guest coming into the den from the back terrace. Rafe was dressed in slacks and an open shirt. Miss Vandergroven was sporting a very expensive beige linen designer suit. Her hair was perfectly coiffed and her makeup expertly applied. Even on a good day, Kendall had never looked so finely turned out.

They both turned to look at Kendall as she approached, Rafe with a clear glance of appreciation that spoke as loudly as a whistle, Miss Vandergroven with a look of pure horror at the crassness of it all. Her green gaze ran up and down Kendall's figure and condemned every curve.

"Hi," Kendall said, smiling at them both. "Excuse my casual attire, but I just climbed out of the pool."

"No excuse necessary," Rafe said, trying not to leer. "Uh, Caroline, this is Kendall McCormick. She's giving swim instructions to the girls."

Kendall grinned. "She is also his brother's ex-fiancée, just so you get me straight," she added. "I'm the one who got left at the altar."

The woman's mouth turned down in a frown. "Pleased to meet you, I'm sure." She offered her fingertips to Kendall, who shook them vigorously.

"The pleasure is all mine," Kendall said in her best "let's all be friends" voice. "Cami has told me so much about you."

Something flickered in the woman's green eyes, and it wasn't delight. "Oh, really?" But she quickly turned away, as though Kendall were of little consequence. "Rafe, darling, I came by in hopes of tempting you away for an early dinner at my place. Just the two of us. Steak and mood music, with no distractions." She slipped her arm through his and smiled coaxingly at him as though Kendall had faded into the wallpaper. "You must come. We haven't had any time to..." She paused just long enough to make sure Kendall got the implications of intimacy. "To be alone in so long."

"What a coincidence," Kendall boomed out heartily, reaching back to pull the band from the end of her braid. "I've been thinking of seducing him myself. He is something of a hunk, isn't he?"

When Rafe and Caroline turned to Kendall in shock, and she smiled, all innocence, as she ran her fingers through her hair, letting it fly free in a cloud around her shoulders and down her back. "The trouble is, he does growl a lot, you know what I mean? That's giving me second thoughts. I mean, is he really as rough as he pretends?" She shivered deliciously.

"Kendall..." Rafe began, appalled and hardly believing what he was hearing.

But she was on a roll. Noting a pack of cigarettes peeking out from Caroline's purse, she snatched them up. "Mind if I have one of these? I've decided to start smoking again. If it kills me, so what?" Without waiting for permission, she pulled out a cigarette and began rummaging for matches. Rafe took two strides across the room and yanked the offending item from between her fingers before she could light it.

Laughing, she shook her head. "Now, isn't that just like you, Rafe." She turned to Caroline. "He does seem to have this antiquated sense of honor or something. Do you know he got me drunk the other night and then insisted on acting the gentleman, even though I was coming on to him for all I was worth. Can you believe it?"

"Kendall..." His face looked like the wrath of God, and his voice rang out with a tone of harsh authority that made her swallow hard, but she was determined to go on. He deserved it.

"After what I've been through, I figure I need a little fun, and since Rafe is being so stuffy about things, I guess I'm going to have to go out tonight and find myself some guys who know how to party. I think I'll start at Giovanni's Bar and Grill and work my way on down to the Kitty Kat Klub...."

"Caroline, would you excuse us?" Rafe ordered in a voice that was not to be contradicted. He grabbed Kendall by the arm, his fingers biting into her flesh. "Kendall and I have some unfinished business to attend to." He glanced at the woman, his face hard as stone. "I'll call you later."

"Is she all right?" Caroline asked rather anxiously as she turned to go, looking back at Kendall as though she were afraid she might have hidden an ax somewhere upon her person. "Do you want me to call someone?"

"I can handle Kendall," Rafe said evenly, glaring at the offending party. "You go on home."

"You see what I mean about the growling," Kendall went on blithely. She bit her lip and made her eyes sparkle. "Now what do you suppose he's going to do—whip me in line? Oooh."

Caroline hesitated, struck by that last comment, but a glare from Rafe had her scurrying out the door. He closed it behind her with a snap, turning the lock as he did so.

"What the hell is this all about?" he demanded, his eyes burning.

"This, my dear Raphael, is about you and assumptions," Kendall shot back, pulling out of his grip and standing toe to toe with him, her chin jutting out.

He stood his ground, eyes narrowed. "What kind of assumptions? What are you talking about?"

"Let's put it this way. What would you say if I were to tell you I was taking up smoking, ready for a good drunk, preparing to take a lover, giving up nutrition and looking into skydiving as a weekend hobby?"

His look dismissed her speech as a frivolous exercise in the pointless. "I'd say you were crazy." It might have been fine if he'd left it there, but he had to go on. "Anyway, I wouldn't allow it," he said sternly.

Her eyes widened. "You wouldn't *allow* it? And just where does your authority derive from?"

His frown deepened. He knew she was intentionally goading him, and he was leashing his anger so as not to fall into her trap. But he couldn't let everything she said pass. "From common sense. You know you can't do things like that in your condition."

Her smile was triumphant. "Ah-ha. And what exactly is my 'condition'?"

He looked uncomfortable. The fact of her pregnancy was something that bothered him a lot, and he didn't like bringing those feelings so close to the surface. "You know what it is."

"Yes. But I want to hear you say it."

He didn't give a damn what she wanted. "I don't want to talk about it."

She would say the words herself if she had to. "You think I'm pregnant."

He blinked at her. "Well, of course, you're pregnant."

Outrage quivered along the length of her. "Does this body look pregnant to you?" she demanded hotly.

Her body looked so tempting, he had to wince when he looked at it, as though he were trying to stare into the sun. "Well, I suppose you're just in the early stages," he said grudgingly, letting his gaze run down the natural line between her breasts until it found itself following the tantalizing shape of her long legs.

"Oh, is that what you think, Mr. Know-it-all?" Her anger brought his attention back to her eyes. "Do you have any idea what happens to a woman's body when she gets pregnant? Even in the early stages?" She didn't wait for an answer. "Her breasts get larger and sore. Her hips loosen and get wider. Her stomach starts to pook out almost immediately, she gets thicker looking, and she gets hungry for things she never thinks of when she's not."

"I know all that. I've got two children."

"Well, if you know so much, tell me this." She placed her hands on her hips. "Does this paint a picture compatible with what you see before you?"

His gaze brushed across her breasts and came back to meet her eyes. "What are you trying to tell me, Kendall?" His look was skeptical. "That you're not pregnant?"

Finally. "Rafe, I've never been pregnant in my life."

He shook his head, but he was beginning to believe her. "Then why did you tell Darren you were?" Anger smoldered in his blue eyes. "And what kind of woman would use a lie like that to trick a man into marrying her?"

She could meet his anger with plenty of her own. "I don't know, Rafe. But I do know that a man who would be tricked by something like that would have to be pretty damn stupid."

Rafe was beginning to feel on less-than-solid ground here. "All I know is Darren thought you were pregnant."

Her eyes flashed amber fire. "Did he now? Then I guess he was even stupider than I thought. Can you explain to me how I was supposed to get pregnant when Darren and I never slept together?"

Rafe's head went back. Her words hit him with physical immediacy that took his breath away. "You mean . . . you never . . . ?"

She sighed, suddenly tired of this. "No, Rafe, we never."

A short, harsh expletive came out of him involuntarily, and he looked away. Relief was flowing through him like a river. She wasn't pregnant with his brother's child. She'd never even slept with Darren. That made all the difference in the world.

Or did it? She was talking, explaining, and he turned back to listen to her.

"I thought I was being very clever," she said softly, avoiding his eyes, her hands clenched on the chair back she was leaning against. "I've watched all the women I know give away their sexuality as though it were going to buy them love. It hardly ever works that way. When I met Darren, I could see that he was used to getting women into bed from the get-go, and that once he'd had them, his interest waned." She smiled and shook her head. "I decided I wasn't going to be one of his bimbos. So I refused to sleep with him. The funny thing is, it worked, in a way."

Turning away, she walked toward Rafe's desk and ran her finger across the smooth wood. "He was crazy to make love with me, wilder and wilder about it all the time. Thinking back, I'm afraid that is probably the only reason he asked me to marry him, though I didn't want to believe it at the time. And when it came down to the wire, he realized there were other fish in the sea."

She turned away, not wanting Rafe to look into her eyes, to see the fear there, the uncertainty. She managed to keep it hidden most of the time, but when she uncovered it, the anguish came back as strongly as ever. Why had Darren deserted her? Wasn't she good enough? Wasn't she pretty enough? Had he decided he could do better? Choose one or all of the above. Why did she still care? She had to blot this chapter out of her life.

Her smile as she turned back to face Rafe was bittersweet. "The price was just too high for him."

Her smile cut into Rafe like a knife. He wanted to kill Darren for hurting her, and at the same time, he was exultant. He wanted her for himself, wanted her here and now with a deep, primitive need that went beyond anything he'd ever felt before.

"Kendall..." He moved toward her, taking her by the shoulders, but as soon as he touched her, whatever he was going to say evaporated. The sweet scent from her body filled his head and her heat set him on fire. All thought came to a standstill, and words meant nothing any longer.

"Kendall," he said again, but it was more of a sigh, half pain, half pleasure, and his hands slid down her arms and then to her hips, pulling her toward him as his mouth lowered to take hers.

She hadn't meant for this to happen, but when it did, she didn't do anything to stop it. She couldn't. Everything in her cried out for him, and she could no more resist the urgency of the demand than she could stop an ocean wave from tumbling her with it.

His mouth was hot and irresistible, and the way he was kissing her was different—hard and hungry—like she'd never felt it before. Her arms lifted to twist around his neck, and she arched against him, shivering as she felt his fingers slide beneath the material on the high cut of her swimsuit, exploring her smooth flesh, his hands meeting to press against her tailbone.

His mouth was on her neck, his tongue making circles, his lips nipping at her sensitive skin, moving against her in a rhythm that set fire to her senses. This was not casual kissing. There was no doubt about what he had in mind.

"Rafe," she whispered, eyes closed, sanity drifting almost out of reach. "Rafe, we can't—"

"Can't we?" He slipped the strap of her suit off her shoulder and slowly peeled it back to reveal her pink-tipped breast. "Why not?"

She sighed, feeling the cool air on skin that was usually covered, knowing she shouldn't let him do this, wanting it just the same. He watched her eyes as he touched the nipple, reacting with a surge of his pulse when he saw the response as she gasped, her eyes widening with wonder. He wanted to watch it all, see every nuance of feeling as he aroused her, feel what she felt when he thrust himself inside her and brought her all the way to the climax she was so ripe for.

Lowering his head, he took the nipple into his mouth and tugged, shuddering as his own need grew harder, more urgent. He was going to go mad if he didn't have her now, he was going to come apart and fly into a thousand pieces if he couldn't feel her cool hand on him, couldn't feel himself moving inside her, couldn't bring her to the mind-shattering moment of complete surrender.

"Hold on," he whispered, swinging her up into his arms. "The couch."

"Daddy?"

They both went very still and held their breaths.

"Daddy? Can Tori come in? She needs her puzzle."

The girls were at the door.

Kendall looked into Rafe's face in horror. She felt as though she'd just been awakened from a nightmare. What was going on here? What was she doing? This was insane.

Rafe's thoughts were more of regret. His hands tightened on her for a moment, but he couldn't think of a way of avoiding the short people at the door. Reluctantly, he released her, letting her slide to get her footing on the floor before he answered his daughter.

"Just a minute, Cami," he said, his voice thick. "I'll be right there."

They looked at each other. Emotion still pulsed between them, but they were drawing away.

"I can't believe we did that," Kendall said softly, staring at him.

"Kendall..." He reached toward her, but she avoided his hand.

"I've got to go," she said quickly, straightening her suit. "I'm late for swim-team practice." She stumbled, almost falling, still dizzy from what they had just shared.

"Kendall, I'll call you."

"No." She shook her head, not daring to look at him. "Don't do that, Rafe. You've got to leave me alone." Looking up, her dark eyes were pleading with him. "Please, don't corner me. Give me time to think."

His hand fell back to his side and she turned and unlocked the door. "Hello, girls," she said cheerfully. "I'm through with your daddy now. It's your turn to bug him."

Without another glance back, she hurried toward the front door.

Rafe leaned back in his chair and stared at the report on his desk without seeing it. He had a raging headache, and there was no way he was getting any work done today. All he wanted to think about was Kendall. Profit-and-loss statements didn't mean a thing to him.

"Mr. Tennyson?" Grace had opened the door to his outer office and was looking in, the light in her eyes full of interest and mischief. "There's someone here to see you. Do you have a moment?"

He shrugged. Why not? This might have something that would take his mind off his obsessions. "I have all the time in the world. Come on in."

Grace turned, and suddenly Kendall was standing in his doorway. Rafe leaped to his feet and came to meet her.

"Kendall. I'm glad you came."

"I thought this might be the best place to talk," she said, avoiding his touch and waiting until he'd closed the door. "We have to clear some things up."

He didn't like the tone of her voice or the look in her eyes. But he certainly liked the rest of her. She was dressed demurely in a white cotton blouse and flowered full skirt, but there was nothing she could do to hide the full potential of her glorious body. She had her hair back in a braid, but wisps flew about her face, framing it attractively. Her lips looked full and kissable. His mouth went a little dry as he thought of what he planned to do once he got a chance. There was a lock on his office door. And an available Do Not Disturb sign.

Escorting her to a chair, he sat on the corner of his desk, facing her, close enough to reach out and take her in his arms. He liked having her there. It put a whole new slant on his day.

"What is it, Kendall?" he said. He could tell she'd come to straighten things out in a way he wasn't going to like, but he was confident he would be able to counter any arguments she might be about to present.

Her dark eyes were wary and she didn't smile. "I came to see you in your office because I thought it might be safer."

He frowned. "Safer?"

"Yes." She lifted her head and gazed at him coolly. "There are phones ringing, people coming and going. We're not really alone."

He was beginning to feel like a wanted man. "What did you think I was planning to do, throw you on the floor and ravish you?" he growled.

She glared right back. "I'd say you were pretty well capable of doing that, yes."

Reaching out, he captured her chin in his hand and spoke down into her face, his eyes hard. "If I wanted to do that, I would have done it by now."

"Ooh," she mocked him softly, her eyes burning into his. "Tough guy."

"Damn right." But he took back his hand, frowning, not sure what he was going to do to turn her coldness into the soft, melting woman he longed to hold. Right now she was anything but soft.

"Okay, here's the deal," Kendall said as crisply as any negotiator. "I'm willing to continue to give your daughters lessons, but I'm not willing to be alone with you again."

His heart went cold. She couldn't really mean this. "What are you talking about?"

"I can't see you again, Rafe. Whenever we're together..." She hesitated, then forced herself to go on. "Something strange and explosive seems to happen."

His mouth twisted. "It's called 'mutual attraction,'" he drawled, reaching out again, touching her hair. "And I kind of like it."

She was scared of him, scared he would do something to tear away her defenses, so she stiffened herself even more, and said coolly, "I don't want to be attracted to you."

He was winding her braid around his hand, looking at the hair, his eyes hooded. "Sometimes you can't help these things."

She had to take a deep breath and fortify her convictions for a moment. "We can help it by staying away from each other," she said at last. "From now on I won't talk to you unless your girls are present."

His mouth tilted in a half grin. "That won't change anything."

Very deliberately, she reached out and yanked her braid from his hand. "I think it will."

"I know it won't. I tried staying away from you when I thought . . . there was a reason I should. But that's gone now." He stared into her eyes with a smoldering look. "And all it did was make me want you more."

For just a moment, her determination faltered. He was so handsome sitting there, so sure of himself. His crystal eyes were like caverns full of mysteries. His mouth was wide and sensuous, his fingers long and lean and strong. For just a moment, she remembered what it was like to feel his body against hers, and there was a catch in her breathing. God, but it was tempting to say the heck with it and let him wrap her in his arms.

But she couldn't do that. She was nobody's one-night stand, and she had vowed to stay away from anything more entangling. She wasn't sure why he wanted her—maybe because of Darren, maybe because she struck a responsive chord in him on her own.

What did it matter? She'd held out for marriage once before and that ploy had blown up in her face. Still, she couldn't see herself settling for anything else. Casual sex had never been satisfying to her. She wanted love. Even if she didn't quite believe in it.

Carefully, she strengthened herself before she spoke again. She was breathing rather hard, but she was still maintaining control. "But you're overlooking one thing," she said forcefully. "I don't want you."

He touched her cheek with the backs of his fingers, stroking gently. "Liar," he said softly.

She stared at him. This was very hard to do, and he wasn't giving an inch. She would have to go to harsher measures. Steeling herself, she said coldly, "What do I have to do to get through to you? Don't you understand? Let me spell it out. I am not going to make love with you. Why should I? I didn't make love with your brother, and I was engaged to marry him."

Finally, she'd hit a nerve. Something in his eyes recoiled, and he pulled his hand back.

She didn't waste a moment. She couldn't risk giving him a chance to regroup. Jumping up, she started for the door.

"I mean it, Rafe," she said from a safe distance. "I don't want a lover. I don't need one. And I especially don't need you around driving me crazy."

He stared at her, his eyes opaque, expressionless, and he didn't move. She hesitated for a moment, disappointed, really. She'd expected him to come after her. But it was just as well he hadn't. Maybe he was finally getting the picture. Turning, she let herself out and hurried down the hall toward the elevators.

Rafe sat very still, staring at the door as it swung closed. What an idiot he was. He thought he'd gotten rid of the problem. But he'd been fooling himself. The baby hadn't been the problem. The baby was a symbol of the problem. The major roadblock was still the same as it had ever been. No matter what he tried to tell himself, the truth kept staring him in the face. She still loved Darren. And as long as she still loved Darren, Rafe couldn't have her.

Seven

Rafe stretched back the chaise longue and adjusted his sunglasses. He had papers strewed all around him, but they were just for show. From behind the dark glasses, he could do just about anything he pleased, and it pleased him to watch Kendall give the swim lessons, no matter what she thought of it.

He was living within the letter of the law on the rules she had laid down. But the spirit was iffy. For almost a week now, he hadn't tried to see Kendall alone. In fact, he only saw her during the lessons. But while the lessons were going on, he saw every bit of her he could.

It was soothing, really, to watch her this way. She had a calm, steady way of working with children, with flashes of humor that delighted them. It was obvious

Cami and Tori adored her. He felt pretty much that way about her himself.

The girls were learning a lot, and he enjoyed watching them chug across the pool like little tugboats while Kendall called out corrections and encouragement. He also enjoyed observing and comparing the different swimsuits she wore every day. The persimmon was his favorite, maybe because he had fond memories of having slipped his hands beneath it that afternoon in his study. But the electric blue was almost transparent, and the black added a sultry allure the others didn't quite have.

At first, Kendall had tried to ignore him, but his occasional caustic comments and off-the-wall bits of humor had made her laugh, and now he was an accepted part of the routine. Cami even called to him to watch when she was doing something especially new and scary.

Progress in his relationship with the girls was going more slowly. Kendall had made a lot of sense on that score, and he'd made up his mind to do something about the way things were. She'd said they needed to communicate and he was sure she was right. The question was, how was he supposed to go about doing it?

Lord knew he tried to do the right thing. He tried to talk to his little girls. He sat them down in chairs at breakfast and attempted some normal conversation, but they wouldn't cooperate. They sat as stiff as truants reporting to the principal. He couldn't get a smile out of either one of them to save his life.

He tried taking them for a ride in the car, stopping at the park, going for ice-cream cones. Nothing worked. It was hopeless. He just wasn't a kid person.

That very morning he had attempted a friendly chat while waiting for the car to come to take them to their piano lessons. Cami had answered in monosyllables, and Tori had steadfastly refused to acknowledge his existence.

The frustration had gotten to him, and though he had refrained from yelling, he had been a little abrupt when he had confronted the younger child.

"Tori," he'd demanded, "can't you say something?"

Cami had interceded as she always did, pushing herself between them. "She doesn't have anything to say."

He'd stared at his oldest child. "Does she talk to you?"

"Yes." The eyes were wide and innocent.

Rafe had spread his arms wide. "When?" he'd asked, bewildered.

Cami shrugged. "When she wants to."

It was the perfect answer. There had been nothing he could say to that. "When she wants to." And she didn't want to. So what was he supposed to do next?

It had finally occurred to him that it might be a woman thing. They were all nuts. And mysterious. And unreasonable. And he was beginning to realize they were already weird by the time they were four and six. No wonder no man could figure them out by the time they were grown and gorgeous.

So what could you do but settle back and enjoy them? That was how he planned to spend a good part of his summer. He only wished there were a way he could extend these swimming lessons. How about four hours a day? Maybe five?

Kendall knew exactly what Rafe was up to. At first she'd resented it. But as she got used to his presence, she had to admit he was kind of fun to have around. And by now, she was surprised at how well it had gone, and how little pressure he'd put on her. The electricity still snapped between them and she knew he was still attracted, but he seemed reluctant to push it, and for that she was grateful.

She was still very concerned about Rafe's relationship with Cami and Tori. She could see that he was trying, but the girls had been hurt too much, too deeply to be ready to risk being hurt again, and they hung back. At one point, Cami told her she liked her Daddy better when Kendall was there, and that made Kendall think she had to do something to spur things along.

She'd majored in psychology in college, and she was a firm believer in acting out and learning from it. If you forced yourself to act nice, pretty soon you would become nice. If you made yourself start the day with a smile, you would be a happier person. It was like training a muscle. If the girls acted as though they liked their father, pretty soon it would be a fact of life. She began to use moments when Rafe wasn't around to drill them in polite friendliness, little things they could say and do to warm the feelings between parent and child. They learned because children are little sponges absorbing everything they come in contact with, but she didn't have the feeling her theories were working very well. Only time would tell. The day Cami told her she loved her daddy would be the day Kendall would know her plan was working.

And how did *she* feel about the man? She wished she knew. She wasn't sure how she felt about anything. In point of fact, the wedding and everything that happened as a result of it had thrown her for more of a loop than she'd realized at first. It was taking time to settle back down again, find her equilibrium. She still didn't know for sure what she wanted out of life.

She knew what she didn't want. She didn't want to throw herself away on a flake like Darren again. She didn't want to find herself in a relationship in which things were bartered with no love behind them. And she didn't want to grab for the first relationship that presented itself, just to prove to herself and the world that Darren had been wrong to leave her. If that meant ending up alone, that was the chance she would have to take. Ultimately, she had to live with herself, no matter what she did.

For now, she was content to keep working, letting the days pass one by one, building up her strength and her peace of mind again, visiting with her parents on weekends. She enjoyed running her swim school, enjoyed the swim team she coached in the evenings, enjoyed the lessons for Rafe's little girls. That was good enough. For now.

"Daddy, Daddy, watch Tori. She's going to do the backstroke across the pool."

Rafe got up off the chaise longue and walked over to the side of the pool as his young daughter flailed her way from one side of the pool to the other, her little face screwed up and eyes tightly shut, even though she was wearing goggles.

"Hey, Tori, that's great," he said, clapping for her when she surfaced again. "Look out turn-of-the-century Olympics. A new star is coming."

Kendall smiled. She'd had doubts at first, but now she was sure Rafe loved his daughters as strongly as anyone could. And he was working at the relationship. Little by little, things were getting better.

The lesson was almost over when a visitor arrived. Kendall noticed the rickety old Jeep drive up and assumed it must be the gardener. She thought no more about it until a voice interrupted them and she turned to find Mrs. McReady storming onto the scene.

"So this is how you are spending your afternoons when you should be in the office with your nose to the grindstone," the woman cried, standing over where Rafe was sitting, her gnarled hands on her hips.

"Mrs. McReady." Rafe jumped up, startled as Kendall had never seen him before. "I didn't see you drive up."

"Of course, you didn't. You're too busy looking at other things." She turned and scowled at Kendall, looking her up and down.

"Mrs. McReady, this is Kendall McCormick," Rafe said quickly, but the lady was hardly listening to him.

"Haven't we met before?" she demanded.

Kendall smiled shakily, hardly anxious to remind her of where and when. "Uh, I can't imagine..."

But the older woman was too sharp for her. "Ah-ha! I remember now. You were the one who came sashaying into the board meeting, pretending to be a slut." She laughed shortly. "You didn't fool me for a minute, young lady. I knew you were right for Rafe. Told him so at the time." She turned back to glare at him. "Glad to see you took my advice. You should try it more often."

Rafe smiled, but she wouldn't let him get a word in edgewise. "Come on girls," Mrs. McReady said, turning to Cami and Tori. "I promised to take you out to my ranch to see the new puppies. Let's get you into the house and into some jeans and sweatshirts. We'll be covering some pretty rough terrain."

The girls scrambled out, each taking one of her hands. Though they were dripping wet, she didn't seem to notice. It was obvious they were well acquainted.

"How are the kittens?" Cami asked, bouncing up and down. "Tori wants to see that little black one again."

"Most of them have new homes by now," Mrs. McReady said as she led them off. "Though I do believe that little black one is still around. If we can find him. He likes to run off into the hills...."

Rafe turned to Kendall as they disappeared into the house. "I didn't plan this," he said. "Honest."

She sighed, climbing out of the pool and sitting along the edge, her feet dangling into the water. She ought to get a move on, pack up her things and get out of here. But she felt a strange reluctance to do that. Instead, she kicked her feet in the water and looked toward the oaks.

Rafe sank back down onto the chaise longue, watching her. She had on the electric blue suit today, the one he could see right through, the one that was loose enough to let her breasts sway a bit, the dark nipples showing plainly beneath the slick fabric when it was wet, as it was now. Looking at her, he wanted to take a bite out of something.

"I've been good, haven't I?" he asked softly, proud of himself.

She smiled, still looking off toward the trees. "Yes, you've been very good. I'm impressed."

"They say goodness should always be rewarded, you know."

She turned to look at him, wishing she could see through the dark glasses into his eyes. "Do they?" she asked lightly.

"They do. So I thought a nice reward would be you going to dinner with me tonight."

"Dinner?" Could he read in her face how much she wished she could do exactly that?

"In a public place," he went on. "With people coming and going, just like you like it."

She smiled, knowing he was trying to bend over backward to make her feel comfortable about it. But she shook her head. "I can't do that."

He grimaced, turning away, then looking back. He'd known she was going to say that, but it still smarted. "Why not?"

"Because I don't want to...to get any deeper in—"

"What are you talking about Kendall? We haven't done anything all that serious."

"Haven't we?"

He stared at her, wondering what that meant. But before he could ask her, there was a shout from the direction of the house. Turning, they saw the girls running for the Jeep, Mrs. McReady close behind.

Rafe and Kendall waved as the little party climbed aboard and drove off, the two girls waving back.

"They seem to like Mrs. McReady a lot," Kendall noted.

"Yes." He wanted to get closer to her, but he didn't know how he could do that with her sitting on the edge of the pool. "Yes, they do like her."

She turned to look at him. "They like you, too, you know."

That surprised him. "What makes you say that?"

"I can see it in their eyes when they look at you. Just in the last two weeks, things have changed a lot."

He wished he could believe her, but as far as he could tell, it was just happy talk. He shook his head. "I don't see it."

She smiled. "You will." Then she sobered. "Rafe...have you heard from Darren?"

He froze. That was a question he'd been dreading lately. "No." He ought to leave it at that, but he couldn't. There was something about her huge, honest eyes that made it very hard to lie to her or to withhold information. "But I do know where he is."

He waited, almost holding his breath, but she didn't ask the next logical question. Finally, he couldn't take the silence any longer. "Do you want to know where he is?" he asked.

She shook her head slowly. "No. Don't tell me. I was just wondering, that's all."

He nodded. Of course, she was. And she always would be. So why couldn't he give up on her already?

Because, because, because...he wanted her. It twisted him, tore at him, burned inside him. He wanted her as he had never wanted anyone or anything before in his life.

But for God's sake, it was just wanting a woman. It shouldn't hurt this much. It shouldn't keep him awake nights. It shouldn't blot out his work, his ambitions, his formerly healthy social life. This was crazy. He was obsessed with her. Did they have doctors to cure this kind of disease? It would be great to take a pill and wake up without her face in his mind. When he'd split with Marci, it hadn't taken over this much of his life. When would it end?

He watched Kendall pack up her things and walk out to her car. He wanted to follow her, grab her, make her understand. But he didn't. It hurt to watch her leave. But it would hurt a hell of a lot more to make love to a woman who was thinking about another man.

Eight

The lessons were going very well and had been extended for another two weeks. Cami was a natural swimmer; everything came easily to her. Tori had to work harder at it, but she was quite a little worker. She usually aimed at goals with a determination Cami could never have conjured up, and things balanced out nicely. And they loved the water. Kendall had become their best friend. They waited for her to arrive and clung to her when she had to leave. She knew they were using her as a mother substitute for the moment, but she was reluctant to do anything to stop it. They needed someone so badly, why not indulge them for a while?

Of course, there would come a time when she would leave. If they became too attached, that might be a big problem. But she would cross that bridge when she came to it.

In the meantime, she was enjoying them. Cami was a ray of sunshine in her day, and she had grown very fond of Tori's serious little face.

"Cami, why doesn't Tori talk?" Kendall asked one afternoon when the younger child had run in with Rafe to find her new goggles.

Cami's eyes took on the usual glazed look that she assumed whenever anyone asked anything personal about Tori. "I don't know," she said without looking into Kendall's eyes. "Cuz she doesn't want to."

"Did she ever talk?" Kendall asked, watching Cami closely.

She nodded. "At our old house she did. Before we came here."

And then Tori was back, so they went on with the lesson. But Kendall thought about what Cami had said. Had it been her mother's death that had stilled her tongue? Or had Rafe scared her voice out of her?

Kendall knew she was going to have to talk to Rafe about it one of these days—and about doing something to help his little girl regain her ability to communicate. She probably needed to feel secure, but she might need professional help, as well.

The best thing about having Rafe around for the lessons was that he was getting to know his daughters better and better and getting to feel more comfortable around them. That was good. It made Kendall feel as though she were contributing something to the process. Of course, she couldn't have cared less if he was around or not.

At least, that's what she tried to tell herself. But somehow, that claim was beginning to ring hollow even in her own ears.

On an afternoon a few days later, Rafe didn't come out during the lesson and Kendall found herself vaguely disappointed. Before the lesson was over, though, she thought she knew why he was absent. The maid came out and began laying a beautiful setting at the table near the pool—lead-crystal goblets, sterling-silver flatware, embroidered napkins, red roses in a Chinese vase. An excited tingle took up residence in Kendall's chest. Rafe had decided to wine and dine her right here, had he? Well, this time she just might say yes.

Rafe came out onto the pool deck just as the lesson was winding up. Kendall was about to let the girls out of the pool. She was up to her waist in the water herself, enjoying its cool comfort on this hot day. When she looked up and saw him looking wonderful in snug corduroy slacks and a blue turtleneck that set off the color of his eyes, her heart gave a little lurch that surprised her. She had just started to smile when she registered that there was someone else coming behind him. It was Caroline, dressed in a long designer gown that shimmered and clung. Apparently, the woman had taken the measure of her competition and had come loaded for bear.

Kendall wanted to sink into the pool and do some underwater laps. And here she'd thought he had meant the table for her. She looked quickly at Rafe, hoping he hadn't noticed. But his smile was just a shade too cocky. He knew, all right. In fact, he'd planned it just that way.

Her chin lifted and her backbone stiffened. She'd never backed down from a challenge yet. "All set for a romantic evening, are you?" she said with a smile that now had to be forced.

"Looks that way," Rafe agreed, his gaze skimming over her bare shoulders. "There's going to be a full moon tonight, you know."

He was baiting her. She kept her smile demure and said, "Then Caroline had better watch out. You know what they say about men like you under the spell of a full moon."

He grinned, but before he could respond, Caroline came up to the pool, blowing kisses. "Hello, darling children. And you, too. . . Candy, isn't it?"

"Kendall."

"Oh. Kendall, of course. Sorry."

The girls had come through the water, kicking their little legs for nice big splashes, to cleave on to Kendall's arms.

"What happens in a full moon?" Cami wanted to know, her eyes huge.

Kendall suppressed a smile and drew them close. "Werewolves roam the streets and witches ride the skies," she told her in a wicked voice. "Little girls beware."

Cami and Tori looked at each other and shrieked in delicious terror, clinging to her for all they were worth.

Rafe laughed, but Caroline didn't approve. "Why, girls, you know very well she's joking. A full moon means romance, nothing more." She glared at Kendall. "Of all the things to tell children."

Kendall shrugged coolly, holding the woman's gaze. "I figure the terrors of the old myths are a lot more benign than the real horrors lurking out in the world these days.''

''Well, I don't condone scaring children. Especially when they aren't your own to do with as you please.''

Kendall raised her eyebrows. Was that a gauntlet the lady had slapped down before her? Lessons were over, especially now. She gathered the children, who clung to her like monkeys, and came up out of the water to stand on the deck.

''And what do you think, Rafe?'' Kendall asked as she shed the children to shake off their water like good-natured collies. If he was going to let this woman talk for him, Kendall might as well find out now. ''Was I out of line?''

Rafe looked from Kendall to Caroline, obviously relishing this. ''I don't know, Caroline,'' he drawled at last, amusement flickering in his eyes. ''Kendall does have a lot more experience with children than either you or I. I think I'll defer to her judgment on this one.''

''Could we stay for the party, Daddy?'' Cami cried before Caroline had time to give Kendall a full-fledged glare. She turned to face this new trial, but before she had murmured more than ''Oh, don't you think...'' Rafe was saying, ''Sure you can. Run in and put on your party dresses.''

Kendall grinned, enjoying Caroline's chagrin.

''Can Kendall stay, too?'' Cami asked in her shrill little-girl voice.

It was as though time stood still. But at the same time, Kendall took in Rafe's cheerful grin and Caroline's look of complete horror. She wasn't going to stay, of course. How could she? That would be like horning in on a date. Tacky. Tasteless. Rude.

But then she heard Caroline's voice whining, "Oh, no, Rafe, she'll drip all over everything," and she began to smile.

"Let her drip," Rafe was saying. "That's what pool parties are all about." He looked into Kendall's eyes. "Would you join us?" he asked.

She looked at Caroline, letting her sweat for a moment. Laughing softly, Kendall shook her head. "No, I'd better get back. I have things to do."

"But you said swim team was canceled tonight," Cami said, pulling at her hand. "Stay, please, Kendall. Tori wants you to."

"Stay, Kendall," Rafe said softly. "I want you to."

She weakened. "I do have a dress in the car I could change into...." she said.

"Yeah!" yelled Cami, jumping up and down. Tori grinned. Caroline rolled her eyes. Rafe laughed. "Go put it on," he told her, "or we'll have to start without you."

This was nuts and Kendall knew it. Caroline had come expecting a romantic dinner with Rafe, and instead, she was getting a family get-together. It was hardly fair, was it?

Well, too bad, her alter ego replied. Caroline is a phony, and despite what she says, she doesn't really like children at all. She doesn't deserve to have Rafe. Just the thought of that woman hanging around, slapping Tori's hand and trying to dictate the lives of the children made Kendall's blood run cold. No, she and the girls were going to have to work on this. Caroline had to go.

Kendall slipped into her soft cotton sundress and brushed her damp but drying hair out around her shoulders, then went back out toward the pool. It was still very light, but the reflection of the late-afternoon sun glistened on the pool water, and the air was soft and warm. She'd beat the girls back and as she stepped onto the pool deck, she realized Rafe and Caroline were dancing to music piped from the house.

For some reason, her gaze became glued to the sight of Rafe's hand on Caroline's naked back. Kendall couldn't seem to pull her eyes away. And at the same time, a hot, ugly feeling rose like bile in her throat. She hated the woman with an intensity that startled her. It was as though something had ripped apart inside her. She didn't want Caroline to have Rafe. And suddenly, something else became crystal clear to her. She wanted Rafe herself.

What? It couldn't be. She faltered, turning to look toward the woods so the couple wouldn't see her face. It was just a momentary pang, a reflex, like wanting a pastry you see in the baker's window. Four steps down the street and you forgot all about it. Right? It would be that way with Rafe. As soon as she and the girls sent Caroline packing, this feeling would fade away.

Now she wished she could escape, but it was too late. Caroline had seen her, had let out a tiny laugh. "Oh, Candy, you've got to come help me. This boy is making me blush."

"It's Kendall," she said loud and clear, but she really didn't expect Caroline to pay any attention. Her gaze went back to Rafe's tan hand on that white flesh, and she shuddered.

Caroline was giggling, and the effect wasn't pretty. "Oooh, don't do that you bad boy," she cooed. "Candy, I'm glad you're here to chaperon. Who knows what this Casanova would do next?"

Her giggle was setting Kendall's teeth on edge, but it didn't seem to bother Rafe. He looked like a cat with cream on his face, about to start purring aloud at any moment.

"Candy, isn't he just the handsomest thing you've ever seen?"

"It's Kendall," she repeated automatically. "I guess he's all right." She plunked herself down in a deck chair, watching them. "His eyes are pretty good. Chin's a little weak, though."

Caroline squealed in protest, but Rafe met Kendall's gaze over her head and grinned. "I think it's time to switch partners," he said, depositing Caroline in a handy chair and reaching out a hand to Kendall. "May I have this dance, lovely lady?"

Caroline was pouting, so Kendall stood and went right into Rafe's arms, thinking only of spiting the woman. But once she'd found herself in Rafe's embrace, Kendall began to realize she'd been a bit rash. She hadn't been aware of just how muscular he was. With his hard body beneath her hands and his warm breath in her hair, she felt as though her knees were going to give way. Gritting her teeth, she tried to think about dental drills and income-tax forms and other unpleasant things just to get her mind off how very good he felt while he led her down around the pool, stopping to drop her into a deep, romantic dip at the far end.

She looked up into his face as he held her suspended above the water. Caroline could be heard lecturing the maid on some point of table setting in the background.

Kendall grimaced. "You could do better," she whispered to him.

He knew exactly what she meant. "I tried better," he said softly, "but she turned me down."

He swung her upright and led her in swaying circles that made her even dizzier than she already was, until they landed back where they had begun, in front of Caroline. Rafe looked into Kendall's eyes and smiled, and she found herself swallowing hard and attempting to smile back.

The girls came out looking adorable in party dresses and Mary Janes, though Tori's were on the wrong feet, a fact Caroline was quick to point out and laugh at, much to the little girl's chagrin. Kendall hugged Tori and helped her correct the situation, then rose to find that dinner was served.

Salmon fillets, rice pilaf, endive salad—the meal was delicious. Caroline did most of the talking, and still managed to eat a second helping of everything in the time the rest of them finished up their first. The woman was grating more and more on the nerves of most of those around the table, but Rafe seemed immune. Maybe, Kendall thought cynically, it was because he was enjoying the tug-of-war going on around him. Or maybe, she thought more moodily, it was just because he was thick as a brick and didn't catch the vibes. Men had a tendency to be that way.

Meanwhile, Caroline got worse and worse as she wolfed down two servings of cheesecake and launched into a thorough criticism of everything about the girls.

"Tori, darling, why do you glower so? And you know, you must make an effort to speak a sentence now and then. I mean, it's ridiculous. And, Cami, do try to keep your hair pulled back more. It's flopping in your eyes all the time, dear. You want to make your daddy proud of you, don't you?"

The only thing Cami wanted at the moment was a license for murder, Kendall was quite sure. She wouldn't have refused one herself.

"You know, Rafe," Caroline went on, waving her wineglass in the air. "What you and I should do is take a cruise. Somewhere—like the South Pacific, just you and me, gone for weeks, away from . . ." She glanced at the girls. "Everything."

"Yeah, that would be great," he said absently, not noticing that both the girls heard him and were staring his way with stricken faces.

Anger flared in Kendall's chest that he could hurt them so carelessly. Didn't he remember how recently they'd lost their mother? No matter what relations were between them, they were panicked at the thought of losing their father for weeks at a time while he went off on a cruise.

"Perhaps your little friend Candy could stay with you while we are gone," Caroline was saying to Cami and Tori. "Would you like that, girls?"

Kendall very deliberately kicked Rafe under the table and glared at him.

He looked at her blankly. "What?" he asked, and it was obvious he didn't have the slightest idea.

Before she could kick him again, the maid came down the walk. "Telephone call, Mr. Tennyson."

"Oh, all right." He threw down his napkin. "I'll take it in the study."

"Hurry back, darling," Caroline cooed, "we'll be waiting."

She'd taken off her large gold bracelet. The clasp seemed to be broken, and she set it beside her water glass before she spoke to the girls in a voice so different from that she'd just used with Rafe, it reminded Kendall of *The Exorcist*.

"You two, elbows off the table." She looked at Kendall, shaking her head in despair. "You might teach them some manners."

"I'm not a governess, I'm a swim instructor."

Caroline took out a cigarette, lit it and took a long drag, muttering about the low class of help nowadays, and at the same time, Kendall saw Cami's little hand reach out and take the bracelet. At first she thought the girl just wanted to look at the pretty thing, but as she watched, Cami and Tori left the table—without asking to be excused—and went to the edge of the pool, as if working on a scheme that they had coordinated between themselves.

"I hope you plan on making yourself scarce fairly soon," Caroline was saying, her voice acidic. "Rafe and I have plans, if you know what I mean."

Kendall nodded absently, watching the little girls. What were they up to?

There was a splash, and then Cami and Tori turned back toward the table. "Oh, no!" Cami cried, her pudgy little hands covering her cheeks. "Oh, Caroline, I think I dropped your bracelet in the pool."

"My bracelet?" Caroline's hand clawed the empty table where the piece of jewelry had been. "Oh, my God, you little brats!"

Leaping up, she ran to the edge of the pool, standing between the two little ones. "Oh, I see it, it's right down..."

The next sounds out of Caroline's mouth did not form words. They were more like shapeless shrieks. Her arms began to flail at the air, as though she might be able to catch something to break her fall. And then she landed in the water with a gurgling splash, sinking like a stone.

And Kendall stood frozen, not doing a thing because she could have sworn that just before Caroline began to fall, she had seen two little shoulders heave into the backs of the woman's knees. On purpose.

Both little girls turned to look at her. "Oh, oh," Cami said.

Kendall went to the edge of the pool and looked down. Caroline was still screaming underwater.

"Wait," she said, finally startled into coming to life. "She's not coming up. I don't think she can swim."

Kendall kicked off her sandals and dived into the cool water without a second thought. Grabbing Caroline around the waist, she pulled her back to the top and lugged her toward the steps. In a moment, she had her there, choking, but all right.

There was more fury in Caroline's heart than water in her lungs. She began screaming incoherently at the girls before she had regained her breath, shaking her fist with anger.

By now, Rafe had returned. "What the hell is going on here?" he demanded, mystified, standing over where Caroline and Kendall sat on the steps, half in the water and half out. "I leave you alone for five minutes and all hell breaks loose."

"Caroline fell in," Cami told him, looking wide-eyed with innocence. "And Kendall jumped in to save her."

"Rafe, Rafe!" Caroline had lost all her sparkle. Her hair was plastered to her face in unsightly strands, and her dress was ruined. She scrambled up and out of the pool and reached for him, soaking the front of his shirt. "Rafe, those little monsters pushed me in deliberately. You've got to punish them right now. Right now!"

Rafe backed away from her, shaking water from where she'd distributed it. "What are you talking about? This is ridiculous."

"They did, they did, Rafe. You've got to believe me."

Rafe stared at her for a moment, then turned to where Kendall was still treading water. "What happened?" he asked.

Kendall shrugged, gave him her wide grin and a wink, then dived to get the bracelet, handing it to Rafe on her return to the surface. Things were moving right along. Caroline was still raging, but she seemed to be leaving, as well.

"I want to get out of here," she was crying. "If you won't punish them ... if you insist on taking their side ..."

Rafe didn't look annoyed so much as bored by the whole thing. "Caroline, these are my daughters. I take their side before anyone else's."

"I want you to drive me home," she demanded of Rafe. "I've never been so humiliated...."

He shrugged. "That's okay. Ben will drive you," Rafe said, signaling to the chauffeur. "He'll bring the limousine around. Why don't you go on out and meet it?"

Caroline went, sputtering and dripping, and Kendall came out of the pool. Rafe handed her a towel and looked at her oddly. "You didn't orchestrate this little moonlight swim, did you?" he asked.

She shook her head in denial. "Not me. But I must say it couldn't have happened to a more deserving subject."

"I see." He nodded wisely, and Kendall decided he wasn't so thick after all.

As the limousine finally drove off with Caroline aboard, Rafe turned to his daughters, both sitting very demurely on the bench, their eyes downcast. "You girls have had quite a night of it, haven't you? I think you'd better go in and get ready for bed. I'll be in later to talk to you about what you've done."

They rose from the bench and started up the walk, but not before throwing Kendall the smallest of glances—each laced with a healthy dose of mischievous smiling.

"They did push her in, you know," she said. "And not that they didn't have cause. But I suppose they have to be reminded of what serious consequences there might have been."

"Poor Caroline," Rafe said, running his hand through his thick hair. "We didn't treat her very well, did we?"

"She didn't deserve much better. What in the world did you have her here for?"

"I told you." His eyes lit up with humor again. "You're denying me female companionship. A man's got to do what a man's got to do."

She shook her head, exasperated. "That's usually the cue for women to run for the hills," Kendall said dryly, beginning to gather her things.

"No." He erased the distance between them and took her wrist in his hand. "You're not driving home in those wet things. You need a hot shower. Some fresh clothes." He hesitated, then added softly, "Why don't you go ahead and spend the night?"

Her eyes widened. "Spend the night?"

"Sure." He touched her cheek with casual affection. "Listen, it's not like that. This house has fifteen bedrooms. Choose one, the maid will make it up for you. After all, you're the heroine of the day. You should have a shower, a fluffy robe, a beautiful room...."

It did sound very inviting. To her own astonishment, Kendall began to consider it.

Nine

An hour later, Kendall was padding down what seemed like an endless hall, wrapped securely in a fat, fluffy white robe and feeling toasty warm from her whirlpool bath. She'd looked in on the girls, and they were both sound asleep. Now there was nothing left to do but go on into her own room and get some sleep.

She hesitated in the doorway, looking back down the hall. She'd been up and down that darn hall three times now, and still no sign of Rafe. She'd even checked his room. What did this mean? Was this all there was? Had he really meant it when he'd told her not to worry?

She couldn't accept that. She listened for a moment. The house had an eerie quiet. It would seem everyone was asleep. Did that mean Rafe had left? Gone to apologize to Caroline, perhaps? Surely not.

But he wasn't around, and that was for sure. Turning from the room, Kendall headed for the stairway. She was much too keyed up to sleep. Maybe she would find a book or something to distract her.

The lights were off downstairs. She felt her way into the library, wishing she had paid attention to where the light switches were in this house. Her hand brushed something filmy and she shuddered. It was probably a lacy throw cloth, but in the dark, shadows were monsters and lacy throw cloths had a disturbing similarity to spiderwebs. Where was that darn light switch?

"Hello there."

She jumped sky-high, gave a tiny, mouselike squeak and turned to run. Shadows that spoke in the dark were worse than spiderwebs.

"Hey, it's only me."

She stopped and turned back reluctantly. That shadow had a familiar voice. "Rafe?"

A small, green-shaded lamp came on with a snap, and there he was, ensconced in a huge wing chair, a drink in his hand.

"Rafe." She put her hand over her heart and took a deep breath. "You scared me. What are you doing here?"

"Waiting for you," he could have said, and it would have been partly true. But he didn't want to scare her off too soon. Smiling, Rafe motioned for her to take a seat in the slipper chair facing where he sat. She looked earthy and seductive in that fluffy white robe. Her legs were bare, and so were her feet. Made a fellow wonder just what other bareness was lurking beneath the Egyptian terry cloth.

"I'm just sitting here in the dark, drowning my sorrows in drink and contemplating my fate," he drawled sadly. Twisting his mouth down, he decided to tease her a little. "Thinking about what it would be like to be married to Caroline."

"Married to Caroline!" The very concept made Kendall roll her eyes and glare at him. He couldn't actually be serious, could he? "Why would you do that to yourself?"

"Well, I don't know, Kendall. You see, I've got these two little girls I don't know what to do with. I'm starting to think I'm going to have to get married to someone who does." Actually, that thought had only begun to nag at him in the few minutes before she had arrived on the scene. Still, he sort of liked the sound of the idea. It seemed mature and farsighted.

But Kendall didn't give any sign of noticing that. She flashed him a stern look. "That somebody isn't Caroline. She doesn't have the slightest idea of how to treat children."

"She doesn't?" He leaned his head back and frowned, pretending to be floored by her logic. "I thought all women knew that instinctively." He sighed. "Well, to tell you the truth, I never could really picture Caroline knitting little booties."

He loved Kendall's wide smile, and there it was again. "This may come as a shock to you, Rafe, but Cami and Tori are beyond the little-booties stage."

"No kidding? I really am out of the loop on this stuff, you know. Why couldn't they have been boys?"

Rafe looked as though he were brooding, his eyes dark and thoughtful, and Kendall realized that she actually felt sorry for him. "What makes you think you would do any better with boys?" she said.

"Boys?" He was startled that she needed to ask. "Boys are easy. They say what they mean and catch balls and get dirty. When they swear, you wash their mouths out with soap. When they fall out of trees, you take them to the emergency room to get their arm put in a cast. When they hit eighteen and talk back, you kick them out to try life on their own. What's not to know about boys?"

Kendall was laughing. "Somehow, I think there might be more to it than that."

Rafe grinned. "Maybe so." And then he sobered, because this was actually a serious problem, one he wasn't too clear on solving. "The truth is," he said, taking a long sip on his drink, "I am concerned about the girls. They do need a mother."

"But you can't marry someone just to provide a mother for your kids."

"No?" He seemed surprised again. "Why not?"

Her great grin was back. "That crazy little thing called love ought to be involved."

"Hey, I thought you were the one who didn't believe in love."

Kendall shrugged and looked away. "I was just going through a phase."

"Ah-ha. So, does this mean you've rediscovered that most passionate emotion?"

Her smile was wistful, and she looked into the darkness beyond the circle of light they were sitting in. "Maybe," she said softly.

Ice settled around his heart as he watched her. He'd known she would get over her anger at Darren eventually. But he'd hoped that sloughing away the rage wouldn't leave behind the love.

Rafe threw back the rest of the bourbon and enjoyed the sting as it went down. He wasn't going to think about Darren any longer. Kendall was a free woman. He could go after her if he wanted to. Darren was history. He had nothing to do with it anymore.

The only flaw in that argument was Kendall herself. She was still too wrapped up in Darren to come to Rafe the way he wanted her to, the way he had to have her. There had to be some way to erase Darren from her mind.

She was talking again. He watched her lips, her white teeth flashing, the shadows deepening her eyes, and he wanted to kiss her so badly, it ran through him with jagged pain.

Kendall looked up and saw the torment on his face before he could hide it. She assumed he was still thinking about the girls.

"It's not easy to lose your mother when you're so young," she said quickly. "You've got to give them time."

"But they've done really well." He shifted his weight and put down the empty glass. "They were a mess when they first came. Marci—for all her faults, she was a damn good mother, and they missed her so much." Funny how her death had blunted the sharp edge of his rage. He could think of her as Cami and Tori's mother now, not the woman who had almost ruined his life. "They were lost without her. And I was scared to death. I had no idea what to do with them."

He remembered how they had looked, so pale and forlorn, holding each other by the hand and staring up at him as though he were about to lock them up in cages. What had Marci told them about him? He couldn't imagine—and he didn't think he wanted to know.

"You are getting better, too," Kendall commented. "Take tonight. When you realized they had pushed Caroline in the pool, you didn't yell at them. You took them aside and discussed rational reasons why they shouldn't have done that. I think you'll find that works most of the time."

"Yeah?" He was pleased with himself. Why not? But he had a long way to go.

"Cami told me something interesting the other day. She said that Tori used to talk before she came." Kendall watched his eyes as she spoke.

"Before they came here?" He lifted his head and stared into her dark eyes. "Really? Then it's me, isn't it?"

She frowned. "What do you mean?"

He shook his head. His face was hard and had a troubled look. "I thought maybe she was just slow to develop. But if she used to talk . . . it must be my fault she quit."

There was pain in his face. Kendall wanted to reach out and smooth his hair back, whisper something soothing, kiss him. "Did you do something that scared her?"

"No." He shook his head, closing his eyes. "She can just sense . . ." His voice trailed off, and he stopped. This was an area he didn't want to get into.

Kendall sat very still, but he didn't continue. "Sense what?" she asked at last.

"Nothing."

"Rafe." She came up out of her chair and came to his, sinking to her knees beside him, her hand on his leg, her gaze soft with concern. "Tell me what it is."

He looked down at her in the fluffy white robe, her hair streaming out around her in an auburn cloak, and his whole body ached to lie beside her. He'd never felt this way about a woman before, not even Marci. This was a need that almost overwhelmed him. But he had to hide it.

"It's nothing, Kendall. I shouldn't have had that drink. It's just about knocked me out." He touched her face with his forefinger and smiled. "I guess that's just the way the cookie crumbles for us weak-chinned guys, huh?"

She laughed. "Rafe, you know I was only making things up to goad Caroline."

"I don't know...." He put on his best woebegone look. "I spent most of the last hour looking in the mirror, trying to see where the flaw lies...."

She took a swat at him. "You did not. You're so vain, you probably have your looks memorized, don't you?"

"Is it real or is it my memory? Only my barber knows for sure." His eyes changed as he looked down at her smile. "What do you think? Do you want to make love?" he asked.

Her mouth dropped, shocked at the sudden switch in subject. "What? No!"

He shook his head sadly. "I was afraid of that. Guess I might as well go to bed, then." He started to reach for the empty glass.

Kendall felt a flutter of panic rising in her throat. "Wait," she said quickly, putting out her hand to stop him.

His eyes were dark and luminous as he looked down at her. "For what?"

She hesitated. She didn't know. It was just too soon to lose him.

"A good-night kiss?" he asked her softly.

Almost shy, she nodded.

He leaned toward her, and she stretched up to meet him.

His lips were cool, and he tasted like bourbon and smoke. She'd meant to give him a simple kiss, one that would let them draw away and laugh and walk arm in arm up to their respective beds. But his taste was intoxicating, and she found her lips parting as though a force of nature was at work, her tongue tempting him in, and when he got inside her mouth, his heat belied the coolness of his lips.

His arms came around her, hard as steel, smooth as velvet, and he drew her up into his lap, his hand sliding beneath the robe, reaching for her bare breast. She felt as though she had been the one who had drunk the bourbon. Her muscles were gone, her arms and legs powerless, and she arched in his arms, giving him her body.

Urgent need was throbbing in him, keeping time with his racing heartbeat, driving him toward something he knew he shouldn't do. But he wanted her so badly. If he could just block off his mind...

Her eyes were closed. Was she pretending he was Darren? Rafe went cold, as though water had been thrown in his face.

"Kendall," he said, holding her close and burying his face in her hair. "Oh, God, Kendall, you make me crazy." Raising his head, he pushed her off his lap. "I have to get out of here before we do something we'll both regret," he said harshly.

And he was gone, striding off toward the stairs, leaving her to gasp for breath and stare after him, feeling cold and all alone. What had gone wrong? She blinked hard, but the answer didn't come to her. The man didn't want her. What else could it be?

Rejection. That was it. Well, she'd dealt with that before. Maybe it was time she took the hint. Maybe there was something about her that was ultimately unattractive to men.

She'd thought Darren loved her, but he hadn't cared enough to marry her, or even to be honest about how he felt. And now the vibes from Rafe were strong and arousing. She'd thought his attraction was a foregone conclusion. But when she tested it, he backed away. Was she misreading signs? Or was there something about her that turned men off?

Standing there, she went through a gamut of emotions, from hurt to sadness to uncertainty to outrage. How dare men treat her like this? It wasn't fair.

She climbed the stairs slowly, getting angrier with each step. Why did he ask if he didn't want her? Why did he invite her to stay the night? Why did he smile at her the way he did, hold her, kiss her...?

No, damn it, she wasn't going to fall back into a huddle and whimper. She wasn't going to be cast along the side of the road without an explanation, as she had been at her wedding. If Rafe didn't want her, he was going to have to explain why.

She'd never made love with Darren, and suddenly she realized the real reason for that. She hadn't wanted to. She'd liked Darren, thought she could spend a lifetime with him. But she'd wanted marriage more than she'd wanted Darren. She had never wanted the intimacy with him that she wanted with Rafe. She wanted to make love with him. She wanted to hold him and love him and sleep beside him. She wanted to wake up in his arms. She wanted him now.

And if he didn't feel the same, he had some explaining to do.

Walking down the hall, she passed her bedroom without a glance and went on to Rafe's, knocking hard.

The door came open, and there he was, shirtless, his dark skin smooth with hair that made her itch to touch him. His shoulders were so wide, the ridges along his abdomen so sharp and hard, and the way his slacks hung low on his hips almost took her breath away.

But he didn't seem to be very happy to see her. A look of pain came over his face. "Kendall..." he began warningly, leaning against the doorway.

He was so beautiful, she almost faltered, but something inside kept her strong. Lifting her chin, she said evenly, "May I come in?"

He hesitated, then stood back and let her enter.

She walked slowly into the room, turning to look at the royal-blue drapes, the light-blue bedspread, the striped pillows, the antique dresser, the pictures. The photographs were of the girls. She wondered for a moment what Marci had looked like, but she imagined it was something like a grown-up Cami. That thought almost made Kendall like the woman.

"Kendall..." he began again, but she swung around and stopped his speech before he had a chance to launch it.

"I came here for a reason, Rafe. I'm puzzled about something, and I thought maybe you could help to clear it up for me."

He looked at her uncertainly, recognizing the flash of anger in her eyes. "I'll try," he said, searching her face for clues as to what she was upset about.

"What I want to know is this." She took a deep breath and folded her arms across her chest, staring him down. "Is this just a little game men play? And if so, how come nobody ever let me in on the rules?"

Rafe shook his head, mystified. "What are you talking about?"

"I've gone all summer with you looking me over like I was on someone's menu and you were ready for a full meal. You give me those hot looks. We've shared a few kisses that sent my thermometer off the scale. You tease me. You entice me. And then when I finally say yes, I want you, let's do it, you yawn and go to bed." Her hands flew out in question. "What am I missing here?"

Rafe gaped at her in surprise. "No, Kendall, you don't understand."

"You're damn right I don't understand. Does it run in the family, or is it me? First, Darren leaves me at the altar, then you leave me standing in the middle of the room with my arms out and my lips puckered. What is this? What am I doing wrong?"

He wanted to laugh, but he held it back because he knew laughter would infuriate her. And she was mad enough already. The term "wet hen" came to mind, but he knew it would be disaster to use it. Besides, he wasn't really sure what this outburst meant. Did she really want to make love? And if so, why now? Why would she want to make love with him when she had never slept with Darren? Did that mean she didn't care about him as much as she had Darren, or that she cared more? Or did it have absolutely no bearing on anything at all?

He went for the last option, not because he thought it was the right one, but because he wanted it to be, because he was through holding back, waiting, letting thoughts of Darren torture him.

But first, how to explain to her? "Kendall, it's not you. It's me. It's my fault. I never meant to make you feel unwanted."

"Then you want me?" she asked bravely, holding her breath and waiting for the answer, staring at the bed because she didn't dare risk watching his eyes.

"Want you?" He was nothing but a mass of pounding want and need, didn't she see that? "Yes, but, Kendall, I wasn't sure if you were ready."

She turned and made herself look into his face. "You can't get off that easy," she whispered, and slowly, very slowly, she pulled open her sash and began to let the robe drop. It fell away from her shoulders, then slipped over her breasts, and finally slunk to the floor in a rush that, to her, sounded like a wave on the ocean. She stood before him, her face hot with blood, her body as naked as the day she had been born.

It was up to him now. She was his, if he wanted her. If he turned her away, she would have to leave the house and never come back again. She wasn't sure how it had come to this. She'd never meant to get here, in this position. But here she was. And it all rested with him. She couldn't read the answer in his eyes. She could only stand very still, holding her breath, and pray.

For a moment, time stood still. He wasn't moving, wasn't coming toward her. She closed her eyes, unable to look at him any longer. If he didn't really want her...

Suddenly he was there, his hands on her shoulders, his voice low and hard. "Don't do this, Kendall. Unless you're ready to take the consequences."

She opened her eyes and stared into his. The consequences were exactly what she wanted.

He read the acquiescence in her face and knew he was lost. He couldn't wait any longer to find out who she wanted, who she loved. A strange, irrational feeling had come over him. Maybe he could make her love him. Maybe he could prove to her that he was the one she really needed in her life. If he just made love to her right, he could show her....

Her body was the most beautiful thing he had ever seen. The shape of her full breasts, the wide, flat nipples, as soft and pink as rose petals, the scent of her warmth—he wanted it all, wanted to touch her, hold her, thrust himself inside her and never come up for air.

The throbbing was pain now, hard and tight and angry, but he ignored it, and when he came to her, it was her lips he kissed, not touching anything else. His mouth clung to hers hungrily, reaching for something he knew he couldn't find, still wanting to know who she loved, needing to have it be him. His hands cupped her face, holding her like a precious jewel, but his senses were aware of her breasts, her hips, the lovely line of her waist, the darkening where her legs met. As he tasted her, he let himself slide into the warm, hot pulse of hypnotic repetition. His hands began to slip down the length of her beautiful neck, fingers massaging her collarbone, then lowering to take hold of the incredibly soft, incredibly tempting shape of her breasts, rubbing, pressing, arousing her until she began to make little gasps of pleasure.

"I'm going to love you, Kendall," he whispered, rubbing his face against hers, his lips against hers, until they both felt raw and vulnerable. "I'm going to love you like you've never been loved before."

It was a promise he knew he could keep, because he felt a swelling of need he had never felt before. It threatened to overwhelm him, but he forced it back, stroking her, touching, squeezing, teasing, determined to bring her to the edge of madness before he gave her the relief she was already beginning to reach for.

Kendall wasn't thinking anymore; she was only feeling. Her hands went automatically to flatten on his hard, muscular chest, the fingertips digging in as though she had needed a place to hold on to him. She could feel his heart pounding beneath her touch, and it frightened her. He was so real, so alive. Could she make him happy?

But there was no time to hesitate. Something inside was driving her toward a goal that was only hazy in her sights. Maybe if she could get closer to him...

She reached for his belt, her fingers trembling as she fumbled with the buckle. He had to help her, but it was her hands that slid in and peeled away his slacks, leaving him as naked as she was, and so beautiful, she could hardly catch her breath.

And then his body was enfolding hers, pressing closer and closer. His kiss was challenging her again, hard and hungry, sending her reeling so that she had to cling to him to keep her head above water.

He lifted her and carried her to the bed, laying her gently on top of the covers. All she knew was that his body was no longer touching hers. She moaned, reaching for him to come back. He returned, lying beside her, running his hand between her thighs, lowering his mouth to take her nipple. She was losing reality, leaving the mundane behind and entering a realm where she had never been.

Her body was a glowing thing, shimmering and turning in a warm tropic breeze, buffeted by the pounding waves of a tropic ocean, soothed by the silver-blue waters of a tropic lagoon. The water cascaded over her breasts and filled her navel with a pool of silver light. It spread itself across her skin like a gentle river, reforming to make a raging rapids race between her legs. She was floating, turning in the current, gasping when the water hit her face. And when she opened her eyes, he was with her, his dark body blocking out the sun, his hands lifting her hips as he touched her lightly, softly, to ready her, stroking, then testing, then pulling her to him for the entrance that sent her spiralling through the waves, reaching for the stars, shooting higher and higher until she had no voice left for crying out, had no breath left for breathing, no energy left for movement and she lay still on the beach where the last, the ultimate wave had cast her.

Their bodies were tangled together in a knot of arms and legs and covers. When Kendall finally opened her eyes to look at Rafe, she started to laugh.

He opened one eye and looked at her blearily. "What's so funny?" he asked, his voice still slurred from what they had just been through. "Are you laughing at me?"

"Never." She took his face in her hands and kissed him over and over, on his eyes, his nose, his temple. "I'm just happy, that's all." She leaned back and looked at him. "Was that the way it always is for you?" she asked with wonder. "I mean, is this something new I never heard of? This was so...so..." She couldn't put words to it.

He smiled and kissed her again. "That was just an appetizer," he whispered, tickling her ear. "Get ready for the main course."

But his arms just held her gently, close and tight, and she relaxed in his embrace. She had no doubts any longer. She was definitely in love.

How had this happened? She wasn't sure. She only knew this was something greater, more fundamental and profound than anything else that had ever happened to her. Rafe was the one—the only one—for her, and she wasn't going to think about anything else.

Ten

The seasons changed. The spring of sadness and regret became the summer of love and fun.

Kendall seemed to be spending every waking moment—and quite a few sleeping ones—at Rafe's house. When she wasn't giving the girls their swim lessons, she and Rafe were driving them to the hills for a picnic or taking the boat to Catalina or spending the day at Disneyland. She rationalized it all as a way to help Rafe get close to his daughters, and it was seeming to do that. But she knew very well the real reason she was doing it was that she wanted to be with him. She didn't want to let him out of her sight. This man she wanted to keep. He was too good to risk losing.

So this was love. It was really very different from what she had ever thought it was. It was like a monster that had a stranglehold on her life. At the same time, it was like a warm bath, all cozy and cuddly like an ermine coat, making her feel classy and protected. Like a scary movie, a roller-coaster ride, a hot-fudge sundae—it was so many things, and she didn't have time to stop and analyze what it was doing to her.

She didn't want to think too much. If she stopped and made plans, set dates, put up goals, she knew she would begin to worry. Rafe had been so reluctant to start this. He had been so hurt by his marriage, she knew he didn't intend to create a love to last a lifetime. This was a summer romance. She'd accepted that. She really didn't want anything permanent any more than he did. Every time she set up permanent boundaries, things fell apart for her. And this was much too lovely to jeopardize with plans.

Mrs. McReady put it into words when she came for dinner one night. "We don't see Rafe much around the office these days," she said crisply to Kendall when they were together pouring out drinks for the table, setting out juice and iced tea on the red-and-white checkered cloth.

"Oh." Kendall tried to smile. She hadn't quite got a handle on how to deal with the crusty woman. "Well, I really think it's important that he have some time to learn to deal with the children."

The older woman stopped and looked at Kendall as though she were a moron. "Oh, is that what you think? And here I thought he was spending all his time rolling in the hay with you."

Red spots appeared in Kendall's cheeks, but she laughed. "A little of that, too, Mrs. McReady," she admitted.

"I'll say." The older woman gestured toward where Rafe and Cami were grilling burgers on the barbecue. "He looks prouder than a tomcat these days. Funny how that sort of thing makes men feel in control."

"I don't know much about tomcats, Mrs. Mc-Ready," Kendall said, attempting to convey a sense of serenity she was far from feeling. "But Rafe is a man who always seems in control." Which was one of the things she liked about him. Say what you will, it was nice to have a man who wasn't rattled too easily, a man she could depend on.

"Well, a tomcat is what Rafe seemed like for the last few years, ever since that marriage of his went bad," Mrs. McReady went on, setting out the cups and folding the napkins. "Only it was a lean and hungry tomcat, the kind that goes through garbage cans and gets into scrapes." She looked Kendall up and down. "Now that's all changed. He's a fat and sassy tom who looks like he loves nothing better than hearth and home these days. And that's what you've done to him."

Kendall couldn't tell for sure whether Mrs. Mc-Ready thought that was good or bad. "And what do you think he's done for me?" she asked, for lack of anything better to say.

"Tamed you down, if that show you put on in the board meeting was any example of how you were." Her laugh sounded like a chain saw hitting a nail in a board. "Lord, you made those old geezers sit up and take notice. Some of them have been on oxygen ever since."

She laughed again, and Kendall smiled uncertainly, sure the woman was only joking. Wasn't she?

Mrs. McReady sobered, sitting down on the bench and motioning for Kendall to sit beside her. "That marriage of Rafe's, that was a sorry business, you know. Marci seemed such a beauty, so delicate and refined. Everyone thought it a wonderful match. He treated her like a queen."

She was silent for a moment, remembering, and Kendall didn't say a word. She'd waited a long time to hear about this.

"Well, perhaps that was where he went wrong," Mrs. McReady went on. "He put her on a pedestal and she wanted to get down in the dirt and roll around and see what that was like. After Cami was born, she seemed to change. I don't know what it was. She had a wildness in her eyes. Wanted something new, she did. And so she went exploring."

Exploring. Did that mean what Kendall thought it meant? Rafe with a wife who ran around on him. It hardly seemed credible. Had the the woman gone crazy?

Mrs. McReady shook her head sadly. "I can remember the days when he would be at the office, calling home by the hour, and she would be gone, leaving the baby with the nurse. That little baby left behind and Marci would be God knows where. It drove him wild with worry."

Kendall took a deep breath, wanting to say something, wanting to protest. This couldn't have happened to Rafe. How hurt he must have been. How angry.

"He tried everything to win her back. But he finally had to leave her. And, of course, there she was, pregnant with Tori. It tore him apart, not knowing what to do. But it was too late to put things back together. They filed for divorce and it was all over."

The story brought up as many questions as it answered, yet Kendall knew she couldn't ask for more details. In many ways, it was none of her business. But she did want to know more about Marci. "How did she die?"

"She was with some man, heading for a skiing weekend in Aspen. Their car crashed on a mountain road. She was always with some man. I confronted her once, said, 'What are you doing to your children, your husband?' She laughed in my face. She said she was too young to be tied down, that life was too short. Well, she turned out to be a prophet in her own case, didn't she? And yet, if she hadn't been chasing around, she would probably be alive today. Funny thing fate is, don't you think?"

Kendall had to speak. "I can hardly believe any woman would be stupid enough—cruel enough—to run around with other men when she was married to Rafe."

"Well, Marci did. And it ruined their marriage."

Her heart ached for him. She wanted to go to him right then and put her arms around him from behind, resting her head against him, holding him close to her heart. But she couldn't do it now.

All the moaning she'd done and feeling sorry for herself because Darren had ditched her, and Rafe had been through something so much worse, but he'd never told her. Kendall was a bit chagrined over that. And in some ways, it made her love him more.

They ate hamburgers and corn on the cob. The girls giggled at Mrs. McReady's silly jokes, and they all had a wonderful time.

But that night when Rafe came into her bedroom, Kendall took him into her arms and loved him with an intensity she hadn't shown since that first night.

"My God, Kendall," he said as they lay back, bodies slick with sweat. "You're like electricity. Like a live wire. I can't keep up with you."

"Only for you," she murmured, her eyes full of how she felt about him. Couldn't he see it there? Couldn't he believe in it?

But he looked away, reaching for a drink of water, and she felt tears stinging her eyes. Maybe he didn't want to see it. After all, he'd been hurt so badly, it was probably hard for him to trust a woman again. He didn't want to see it because he didn't want this to be a long-term situation. Like Mrs. McReady said, he was a big old tomcat, and tomcats were notorious for restlessness.

She turned and buried her face in her pillow, not wanting him to see the sadness there. She'd found the man of her dreams, only his dreams were made of different stuff.

The girls were blossoming. They hardly resembled the sad, scared twosome Kendall had seen hiding in the bushes the first day she had come here. But Tori still didn't talk. And Kendall had noticed something that disturbed her. Rafe seemed to like Cami best.

Maybe that was just a little harsh. He was kind to Tori, smiled at her, gave her presents. But it was Cami he reached for, Cami he joked with. And when they went places and paired up, it was always Cami with Rafe and Tori with Kendall.

She supposed it might be because Tori didn't respond the way Cami did. The younger girl was still and shy and serious. And her silence made him nervous.

But Kendall remembered what he had said to her the first night she had stayed with him. Something about Tori's silence being his fault. That she must sense something. He hadn't mentioned it again.

She brought it up to him one night when they were getting ready for bed. She was sitting at her dressing table, combing out her long hair. He came up from behind, kissing her neck. Sighing, she leaned back and smiled at him.

"The girls expect you to take them to the ballet next Saturday, you know," she reminded him. "I got the tickets."

"The ballet?" There was a look of panic in his eyes. "Aren't you coming?"

She grinned. "No, I've got a swim meet in Santa Barbara that weekend. You're going to have to handle this one on your own."

"The ballet." His voice was choked. "Oh, my God. All those women in tutus bouncing up and down and the men in stockings going tippy-toe. You really expect me to sit through that stuff?"

"Watch out or we'll have to sign you up for Daddy and Me ballet lessons." She picked up a brochure and tossed it to him. "Cami is crazy about the idea. See the picture of the father on pointe, right alongside his little girl? She wants to cut it out and put it up in her room."

Rafe moaned. "You're going to save me from this, aren't you? If you don't, I'll be the one running away from home."

Kendall grinned. "It's nice to know we have something like this to hold over your head," she said smugly, then continued, mimicking a deep, masculine voice. "We've got you over a barrel, Tennyson. From now on, you are in our power."

But he wasn't listening. He'd had an idea. "I know what. I could buy out this place. Change all the classes into judo lessons. Daddy and me and a jump kick. How would that be?"

"Rafe..."

"Do you think we could get it through escrow by next week? I'm sure the girls will prefer judo to ballet lessons if you just give them a chance."

"Give it up, Rafe. Cami has already sent away for toe shoes. You're stuck with girls, whether you like it or not."

He was grumpy but resigned. "I like girls just fine," he protested. "If only they would do fun things instead of this boring girl stuff."

Kendall rose and kissed him. "You are getting to be a real daddy, aren't you?" she said softly, half proud, half marveling.

His grin gave evidence that he was actually pretty pleased with himself. "Yeah, I think so. It's not as hard as it seemed at first."

Her smiled faded. She hesitated to bring this up, but it had to be dealt with. Steeling herself, she went on. "You treat them differently, you know," she told him.

He looked at her blankly. "What do you mean?"

"I mean, you feel free to joke and play with Cami. But I never see you doing it with Tori."

His eyes darkened. "It's sort of hard to joke with Tori. She doesn't joke back."

"True. But, Rafe, it's more than just the joking. You give the impression of...of wanting to be with Cami more than with Tori. Of liking her better."

Kendall could see his knuckles whiten as he gripped the bedpost. A pulse was throbbing at his temple. He was making every effort to control himself. "Don't be ridiculous," he said evenly. "That's not true."

"I don't want to think that it's true. But I can't help but wonder what Tori thinks."

He turned, rummaging through a drawer for a handkerchief. He wasn't meeting her eyes any longer. "You're imagining things," he said gruffly.

He started into the next room, but she followed him. Now that she had brought this up, she wanted to get as much out in the open as she could. She didn't want to have to push this issue again.

"It concerns me that Tori still doesn't speak. Maybe it's time to think about professional help for her."

Rafe turned, running his hand through his hair and leaving it wild. His gaze flickered from her to the door and back again, as though he were planning an escape.

"A therapist?" He shook his head dismissively. "I've had dealings with them before. They didn't do a thing a witch with a divining rod couldn't have done better."

She was surprised. "You were in therapy?"

"No," he said, starting for the door. "Not me."

And that was the end of that conversation. That night, for the first time ever on a night when she had stayed at the house, they didn't make love, though they slept side by side in his soft four-poster bed.

She knew they had to get to the bottom of the Tori problem or it would poison more than their relationship. Watching over the next couple of days confirmed her fears. No matter how hard Rafe worked to mask his feelings, it was obvious he preferred being with Cami. And it broke her heart to see Tori's serious little face as she watched the two of them together.

She had to do something. The direct approach hadn't worked. Maybe if she found out more about what their family had been like when Marci was alive, she could gain some insight and get some ideas.

She waited until a night when their lovemaking had been sweet and satisfying, and as they lay together, she went up on one elbow, looking over him, and tracing a pattern on his chest with her finger while she whispered in his ear, "Tell me about Marci."

His head jerked back. "I don't want to think about Marci."

Her hand flattened on his chest and she took a deep breath. "Rafe, do you love Tori?"

Rafe was silent for much too long. He turned to stare at her, his face as hard as if it had been carved from stone. This was a question he had never asked himself, and he was actually rather surprised at the answer. "Yes," he said simply. "I love Tori."

Relief tingled to her fingertips. What would she have done if he had said no? "And you want to help her, don't you?"

"Of course."

Kendall reached for him eagerly. "I want to explore what we can do to help Tori, Rafe. To do that, I really think I have to know about Marci."

He was tense, clenched like a fist, and for a moment, she thought he was going to get angry and storm out. But little by little, he began to relax. And finally he agreed with her.

"You're probably right." He felt almost physical pain in releasing this old news from his memory, and it showed on his face. "This isn't going to be easy, Kendall. I hate dredging this stuff up. But if it will help Tori ... You might as well know the truth."

"Rafe, I'm really sorry to make you do this. I know how much it can hurt to go over old pain...."

He took both her hands in his and held them. She was talking about Darren, he thought. Would a day ever come when she could bring him up without the sadness?

"Okay, here goes. Marci was a butterfly who turned back into a caterpillar. I married a lover and a friend, and I ended up with a monster. I never understood why. And believe me, I thought about nothing else for a few years."

He paused, remembering. "The first year of our marriage was all right. She didn't want to work, and I didn't encourage her to. I sort of liked the thought of her waiting for me at home all the time. And when she had Cami, I thought..."

He shook his head, and the smile that curved his lips was bitter. "Well, what difference does it make what I thought? What happened was, she changed completely, as though something had gone unbalanced in her. She started going off and leaving the baby behind. And then came the day..." He stopped and gripped Kendall's hands more tightly, still staring into space, his voice a monotone. "I came home unexpectedly and found her in bed with the boy who cleaned the pool. And I realized things had gone too far."

He was quiet for a moment, and Kendall wept inside for him. She knew how important control was to Rafe. To have lost control of his life because his wife was irrational must have been a horrible experience.

"It was a hard time," he said at last, going on, his voice strained. "I nearly went out of my mind for a while. I wanted to kill every man she'd been with." He turned and looked into Kendall's eyes, his own a pale silver-blue. "You know what I mean? Go out and kill them with my bare hands. At times, I wanted to kill her."

"But you didn't."

"No." He shook his head slowly. "I didn't. I kept telling myself she was sick, that there was something really mentally wrong with her. I called doctors, hired therapists, put her in clinics. Nothing helped. And I finally realized nothing was going to help until she wanted it to. And she never reached that point. She liked what she was doing." He stared into Kendall's eyes as though he might find the answer there. "That was what I couldn't understand. It was so degrading, to her, to me, to Cami. And she liked it."

Giving up on finding truth in her eyes, he turned his attention to Kendall's hair, picking up a strand and beginning to play with it. His voice was soft as he added, "The last straw came when she got pregnant with Tori."

Kendall gazed at him, mouth slightly open, dreading what she would hear next. He looked into her face again, though she could see it was very hard for him. But what really gave his anguish away was his voice. "I knew it wasn't my baby. I hadn't slept with her for months."

Kendall closed her eyes. "Oh, Rafe."

"That's why I treat Tori differently from Cami," he said, his voice breaking. "I don't want to treat her differently. I like her. Hell, I love her. But every time I look at her..."

Kendall reached out and wrapped him in her arms, pulling his head to her breast, rocking him, tears streaming down her face. They would fix this somehow. She was sure of it. But it would take time, and every time she thought of that silent little girl standing all alone, waiting, her heart broke.

"Kendall, watch this!"

Kendall turned to see Cami leaning out into the spray the sailboat was kicking up as they skimmed along the water. "Hold on tight," she called back, holding her hair to keep it from slapping her face. "We don't want anybody overboard."

"That's okay," Cami cried. "I can swim now."

Kendall laughed and shook her head, then turned back to watch Rafe and Tori. He was manning the rudder with the little girl in his lap, teaching her how to hold the smooth piece of wood, whispering in her ear. It gave Kendall a glow to see them that way. Rafe was trying so hard.

But that was the trouble. It still felt like trying. He had yet to arrive at the point where it came naturally.

Still, what could you say about a man who tried this hard? He had his rough spots and his quirks, but all in all, the more she knew him, the more she loved him.

The lessons were over. The end of the summer was approaching. And with the end of summer came that old black hole. What was her future? She wasn't any closer to knowing than she'd been for months.

"But we'll miss you," Cami had said when she'd told her she wasn't going to be coming every afternoon any longer. Tori's eyes had filled with tears.

"Hey, don't worry you two." Kendall had gone down on her knees and put an arm around each of them. "Your daddy is putting you on my swim team. I'll see you at workout every day."

She'd talked Rafe into it. "They'll be having very busy days, and swim-team workouts will help them get rid of some of their extra energy at the end of them. It's a novice team, made up mostly of kids like them. They'll make new friends. I think they'll like it."

"They'll like anything as long as you're involved," he said, threading his fingers through her hair. "And I think it would be a good idea. Lately, they've been starting to wander a little farther afield than I like. When I get home in the afternoon, they're off in the woods or down by the street. It would be good to have somewhere structured for them to go every afternoon when I can't be here to watch them."

Sometimes Kendall had to ask herself if she'd had an ulterior motive. After all, putting them on swim team meant tying herself to the family again. And in many ways, she wanted the children nearby almost as much as she wanted Rafe. But it really was for the best. Honest.

"Are you sure it's every day?" Cami looked at Tori and shrugged. "That might be okay."

"It will be more than okay. You'll come straight over to the pool after school and your daddy will bring Tori. We'll all be together again."

Cami's face wrinkled up. "Do I have to go to school?" she asked. "Tori will miss me." An idea hit her like the proverbial light bulb. "I know, Tori and me can come and help you at the swim school instead. I could watch the babies, and Tori could sweep the floors...."

Kendall laughed. "You little con artist. Did you really think you were going to sell me on that one?"

Cami looked just a bit sly. "Maybe," she said.

"Maybe not," Kendall shot back. "You'll go to school, and Tori will go to preschool, and then you'll both come to swim team."

"But it won't be the same," Cami wailed, clinging to her.

And Kendall had to admit, Cami was right. It wouldn't be the same at all. And that scared her just as much as it did Cami.

Summer was almost over, and she had a feeling that this was a summer romance, not one meant to last into the dark days. What was going to happen once the children were in school? Was Rafe going to go on some of those business trips he'd been talking about? Would he forget to phone her when he came back?

Call her gun-shy, but it had happened to her before. And the thought of it happening this time twisted a knot in her stomach. She couldn't stand to think of losing him.

So she leaned back into the wind, letting the sun wash over her face, and enjoyed the sail. After all, this might be one of the last chances they would have to share a time like this.

Rafe stared at the well-polished surface of his empty desk. He'd come to the office for some peace in order to get his head together. He had to think things through. What was he going to do about this Kendall thing?

It was good here. The piped-in music was soft and soothing. He was surrounded by highly polished wood and brass and inch-thick carpeting. No one was asking him to tie ribbons in their hair. No one was expecting him to emote, to empathize, to agree on anything. He could lean back and let the marvelous functioning of his brain take over and solve this for him.

Yeah, he was going to get to the bottom of this dilemma in no time. No time at all. He stretched back in his chair and let his mind go.

It took him fully five minutes to realize he wasn't getting anywhere. His marvelous mind was a blank.

Okay, he was a man of action. Maybe he needed a pencil in his hand in order to get the juices flowing. He dug for one, found several and picked the one with the sharpest point.

He was also a man of organization. Maybe he should get his thoughts organized. Pulling out a piece of paper, he drew a line down the middle—promptly breaking the wonderful sharp point and needing a replacement—and labeled one column Pro the other Con. It was time to balance the books and figure out just how seeing Kendall had affected his life.

Okay, pro was good things, like happiness and lovemaking and someone who laughed at his jokes. Con was…being tied down, and wondering if he could trust again, wondering if she still thought of Darren. But he couldn't write those things down. He sat for another five minutes, staring at the piece of paper. There had to be a way to quantify these things. Any moment it would come to him. And when it did—

"Mr. Tennyson." Grace poked her head through the doorway and glanced in. "I'm sorry to disturb you, sir, but Mr. Clinton of Clinton Industries is on the line. They are so upset that you turned down their offer, they would like to wine and dine you until you change your mind. Mr. Clinton wants permission to send over a first-class ticket to Las Vegas for Saturday morning."

He blinked. Tickets to Las Vegas, huh?

"Tell Mr. Clinton I'm very sorry, but I've got to go to a Daddy and Me Ballet night Saturday. Maybe some other time."

"Oh." Grace enjoyed getting that little tidbit. Her eyebrows rose, and she smiled, thinking of him at the ballet with the girls. "Well, if you say so, sir."

Grace disappeared, and Rafe leaned back again. Tickets to Las Vegas. Penthouse suite, no doubt. Dancing girls, rolling dice, complimentary drinks. It didn't even tempt him.

Did that go in the pro or in the con?

He stared at the paper for a bit longer. The piped-in music was really getting on his nerves. He should make a memo to get rid of it.

His door opened again and a beautiful, curvaceous redhead stepped into the room. She was wearing a skirt so tight, it looked like plastic wrap, and a fitted top that allowed for a lot of overflowing. And overflowing seemed to be what she did best.

"Oh, hi, listen, Grace wasn't at her desk so I took a chance and just looked in, because you haven't been here much lately and I didn't know... I came to see what you wanted." She smiled with what had once been called a come-hither look.

Rafe had to cough to cover the choking sound in his throat. "What I wanted?" He stared at her generous proportions. Was it his imagination, or was this perfect stranger coming on to him? "Wh-what do you mean?"

She leaned against the chair, giving him an even better view of her attributes. "I'm Tracy. I'm the new lunch girl. I'm taking orders for the deli. They tell me you usually want roast beef on rye, but I thought I'd check, just to make sure."

"Oh, no, roast beef on rye will do fine." His voice sounded just a little high, but maybe she wouldn't notice.

She batted her very long eyelashes. "Are you sure there isn't anything... special... I can do for you?"

Lord, he must be dreaming. Maybe he was fooling himself. Maybe she was really just a nice girl who didn't realize how she came across. Maybe he should take the good-old-uncle approach.

"Do you have a boyfriend, Tracy?" he asked as jovially as he could.

"Uh, not really. Well, kinda," she answered. "But I'd dump him in a minute for you, Mr. Tennyson," her big green eyes said loud and clear.

Okay, there was no more question about it. She was coming on to him. He grinned to himself. He still had it.

The question was, did he want it?

Sighing, he shook his head and looked at her with nostalgic regret. "Actually, I don't think I want anything today, Tracy. Thanks just the same."

Her face fell. "Are you sure I can't talk you into anything?"

"Nope. I've got a Daddy-and-Me-Ballet date to think about."

She left, and he found himself humming along with the formerly despised music. Life was good, wasn't it?

But where the hell was Grace, and why wasn't she protecting him from this sort of thing?

He got out his chart again and doodled a picture of a monkey in the corner. Kendall. Commitment. Going out on a limb. Risking everything. Trust. He couldn't seem to bring all those elements together in a coherent package he could deal with. How was he going to come up with a solution if he couldn't even articulate the problem?

The door opened again and George Mooney from Applied Engineering waved to him from the doorway.

"Hey, just thought I'd bop in and see if you wanted to go along. Got tickets to the Dodgers game on Saturday. A bunch of us are going together. We're going to dinner before and out to party after. Remember those all-night poker games we used to have? What do you say?''

"George, I'd love to. But you see, I've got these two girls to deal with that night...."

"Two girls! Bring 'em along, the more the merrier."

Rafe frowned. "George, these are my daughters I'm talking about."

"Oh." George looked as though he'd just swallowed a bug. "Well, some other time, then."

The dust had barely settled from George's departure when Grace stuck her head in again. "I'm back."

"Thank God. Guard the gate, will you? All kinds of riffraff is getting in."

"I will, Mr. Tennyson, but...we've got those applicants here, ready to be interviewed. Three lovely young ladies. Can you see them now?"

Rafe stared at her. Was this a nightmare? Was he being tested by some higher source?

"No, I cannot see them now. I'm trying to do something." He sighed. "Listen, Grace, I trust you implicitly. You interview them and decide which one to hire. I'm busy."

"Very well, sir." Grace grinned. "But you do realize this little chore goes under the duties of administrative assistant, not secretary."

"So?"

"So, administrative assistants get paid more. I just want you to keep that in mind." She grinned and vanished.

Rafe pulled out his paper and glared at it. This was turning out to be a lot tougher than he had thought.

He had to exert a little discipline and make himself think. How did he feel about Kendall? How sure was he of how she felt about him? And what the hell was he doing, trying to analyze this? He'd sworn he would never get really serious about a woman again, and he had kept that pledge for four years. Then he'd been bowled over by Kendall. Okay, he'd wanted her badly. And finally, they'd found a way to handle that. He'd assumed the hot flush of desire would fade pretty quickly and he would be ready to move on, like he always was after a couple of months.

But something had happened this time. The feeling wasn't going away. In fact, if anything, it was getting stronger and stronger. And that made it more and more important to know how she really felt.

He got up and began to pace the office. Women. Who could understand them? He couldn't think about this. It was making his brain hurt.

And Kendall…Kendall with the beautiful body and the great swimming technique, the swim school, the great teaching abilities. She was so good with kids. She handled those classes like a conductor before an orchestra. If more people knew about the service she offered, she'd have them lined up for blocks…. Hey, wait a minute. He frowned. An idea was coming to him. A workable, viable, wonderful idea. Yes. Yes, it could work.

Dashing to the desk, he picked up the telephone receiver and stabbed in a number. "Hey, Conan? Get over here right away. I've got an idea for swim-school franchises that'll knock your socks off."

He slammed down the receiver and went back to jotting down figures. This was where it was at, not moaning about feelings and trying to pin them down. Feelings would have to take care of themselves. What would be would be. He was in his element again. Damn, he loved business.

He hardly noticed when Grace entered the office again.

"This just came for you, Mr. Tennyson," she said, laying a postcard in front of him.

He didn't look up at first, still writing down numbers and ideas like crazy, but when he did, all other activity stopped. A postcard from Brazil. It could only be from one person.

Gingerly, he picked it up and read the back. "Hey Rafe, how's your bod? Summer in Rio is a blast. Will be home by Christmas. Thanks for everything. Darren."

With his free hand, Rafe slowly crumpled his pro-and-con chart into a ball and threw it into the wastepaper basket. There hardly seemed to be any point any longer.

Eleven

Kendall drove out from work that afternoon and found no one at home.

"Mr. Tennyson went in to the office," the maid told her. "And the girls are playing out in back."

A trip to the back found no sign of the girls. She turned, looking everywhere, even the pool. Then a flash of something moving caught her eye. Someone was out running through the stand of aspen at the back of the property. Curious, she began the long hike out.

The day was hot, and sweat was beginning to run itchy beads down her tailbone. Small flies buzzed around her face. She was just starting to doubt the wisdom of this venture when she saw a child running through the trees. It was Tori.

Kendall almost called to her, but thought better of it. Maybe she should get a look at what the girls were up to before making her presence known.

She walked softly, avoiding twigs and rustling leaves. And there they were, two little girls bent over something in a picnic basket, cooing as though they'd found a baby.

She took another step and cracked a small branch, sending the girls flying in two directions.

"Cami. Tori. It's me, Kendall."

Sheepishly, they returned. "Hi, Kendall," Cami said, waving. "What are you doing here?"

"Wondering what's in the basket. Are you going to show me?"

They exchanged anxious glances, and Tori bent down to pull the top open. Inside was an adorable tiger-striped kitten, about two months old. It poked its little pink nose up and meowed piteously.

"Who is this?" Kendall asked, reaching in to pick up the beautiful little thing. Its purr could have vibrated leaves off trees.

"Ricky Ticky," Cami told her anxiously. "But don't tell Daddy we have him, please, Kendall. He'll never let us keep him."

"Where did you get him?"

Cami jumped up and down excitedly. "We found him when we were playing by the creek."

His fur was soft as silk. "He might belong to somebody."

"Uh-uh. He was skinny and scared when we found him, and his paw was hurt."

It seemed to be okay now. Kendall smiled as he tried to lick her nose. "How long have you been keeping him out here?"

"Since the day we went to Knott's Berry Farm."

Kendall was aghast. "That was over a week ago. And you've been feeding him?"

"Only things we find in the garbage. We didn't steal anything from the kitchen, honest."

"But he probably needs real cat food."

"I know. But we don't have any."

That could be quickly remedied.

"You won't tell Daddy, will you?" Cami begged. "Promise?"

Kendall remembered. Daddy had said no kitten. She gently lowered the little cat back into the basket and shut the lid. This was not going to be an easy one. She turned back to face Cami and Tori.

"I'm sorry girls, I can't promise you that. But I will help you feed this poor little thing."

That didn't satisfy them, but it would have to do. She led them back to the house. Their worried little faces were puckered with dread. And she could hardly blame them. Rafe had been adamant about not letting them have a kitten.

She ran to the store to get supplies and luckily got back before Rafe got home. She gathered the girls, and they took the food out to the hiding place and watched the ravenous little beast have himself a feast.

It was the cutest little thing, bouncing on stiff legs as though it were going to attack. And it seemed to be healthy. Of course, a veterinarian should check him out. But what was Rafe going to say?

Rafe got home just before dinnertime. Kendall went out to meet him, armed with all the arguments she had worked up about how children need pets. But one look at Rafe's face stopped the words in her throat.

"What is it?" she said, drawing back and staring at him. "What's happened?"

Without saying a word, he reached into the inside pocket of his coat and pulled out the postcard. He hesitated only a few seconds, then handed it to her and watched for her reaction.

She held it in her hand turning it slowly, knowing without looking who it was from. She read the message. "Same old Darren," she said, but even to her own ears, her attempt at lightness sounded strained. She knew her face had paled. No matter what, the man had affected her life and she wasn't completely free of an emotional reaction at the thought of him.

She looked up and straightened, surprised at the black anger in Rafe's eyes. "What is it?" she asked quickly. "What's wrong?"

He turned, still having uttered not one word, and walked into the house. She stood where she was, staring after him, completely at sea.

Dinner was a time of tension. Cami and Tori were worried about Ricky Ticky, and Rafe was upset about something Kendall couldn't quite put her finger on. It had to be about Darren. But what could it be?

It wasn't until they'd put the girls to bed that they had time to talk.

Kendall had gone to bed first, leaving Rafe to make some phone calls. When he came up to her room, she was in bed reading, her hair in a loose braid. He stood in the doorway of her room, looking at her as though he had never seen her before.

Kendall put down the book and frowned. "What are you so angry about?" she asked as he came in, closing the door behind him.

He walked over slowly and sat on the side of the bed, his blue eyes dark and haunted. "You still love him, don't you?" he said evenly.

"Who?" Shock reverberated through her. "Darren?"

He just waited.

"Oh, Rafe, no." She could almost laugh. "I don't love Darren."

"I saw your face when you read the card."

"Rafe, that wasn't it at all. It was like a slap in the face to hear from him again. After all these weeks, he'd kind of drifted into unreality to me. Seeing his handwriting brought him back as something that had to be dealt with. There really is a Darren. He really did promise to marry me and then left me standing at the altar. It isn't all a bad dream. I can't change that. It really happened, and it's going to affect me emotionally for a long time. But love him? Rafe, I never really loved him."

He started shaking his head before she was finished. "Kendall, I know you, and you aren't the type of woman who marries a man she doesn't love."

Kendall reached out and took hold of his shirt. "What kind of woman do you really think I am?" She searched his stormy eyes. "Don't set me up as some paragon of virtue, Rafe. I had an ulterior motive for wanting to marry Darren. I'm not proud of it, but it's true. I liked him fine, yes, but mainly, I just wanted to get married."

"He let you down."

"Yes, he let me down."

"So why haven't you been trying to find someone else who wants to get married?"

"Because my priorities have changed. I've decided getting married isn't the most important thing in the world, after all. I took a shot at it and got slapped down. And that was enough for me." She shrugged. "Some people just aren't meant to get married. Maybe I'm one of them."

He merely stared at her, and she felt chilled. She pulled away from him, watching his face, dreading his mood. "Rafe, how can I convince you? I don't love Darren. I don't want Darren back."

His eyes didn't change, but he tried to smile. "I wish I could believe you," he said so softly, she could hardly make out the words.

He began to remove his clothes, and she pulled back the covers to welcome him in. Their lovemaking was slow and tender. She tried hard to prove with her body what hadn't seemed to convince him with her words. She almost felt that she'd succeeded. He held her close, and she luxuriated in the pure affection she felt.

They talked softly in the dark. He recalled memories of Darren, things that had happened when they were boys, times Darren had been in trouble and he'd bailed him out.

"The thing about Darren," he admitted to her at last, "is that he makes me feel so damn guilty. I always feel as though I've stolen something from him."

"You mean the business?" She'd heard some of this from Darren's point of view and knew there was some bad feeling on this score.

"Yes. I've got the business, and Darren's got nothing."

"He's got a trust fund that supports his playboy life-style," she reminded him.

"I know. And he had every chance to join the firm. But nine to five were just not his hours. He never wanted to join us. So now he's a playboy. But don't for a moment think that he's a happy man."

She nodded. From the vantage point of hindsight, she could see these things clearly herself. "I know what you mean. And I think you're right."

"I've always felt that I got the big end of the stick, you know."

Reaching out, she took his face in her hands and looked at him wonderingly. "So what is this all about? Have you decided to give me to him to make up the difference?"

"No." Rafe laughed at the absurdity of the idea, stretching up to kiss her mouth. "Of course not."

She stroked his cheek. "Still, it's not your fault. He's a grown man, and he's made his own decisions. Let it go." She kissed him again and sighed. Since it was time to unburden, she had a few secrets of her own to share.

"Forget Darren. I've got something to tell you."

Rafe went very still. "What is it?"

She took a deep breath. "Do you know that psychologists say keeping a pet is a healthy thing for a child? It teaches responsibility, develops nurturing. Don't you think it would be a good thing for the girls to have a kitten?"

"A kitten?" His voice sounded completely uninterested. He was still immersed in the other things they'd been talking about. "No, I don't want any animals around here. They tear up things and make a mess."

"What if they promise to keep it out of your sight at all times?"

He turned toward her in the dark. "What's going on, Kendall?"

"Okay, here's the truth. The girls have found a kitten and they're hiding it in the woods. They take it table scraps. They adore it, and it's really cute. I think you should let them bring it home."

His voice was deceptively calm. "You've been out to see it?"

"Yes. It's really a darling little thing. Once you see it..."

"You mean, you were in on the lie?" All the anger he felt over the situation with Darren was finally finding an outlet. "You've encouraged my daughters to lie to me?"

"Oh, no Rafe. It's not like that. They didn't tell you only because they were afraid—"

"And you think that's normal, for them to be afraid of me? And all over a damn cat." She saw him getting up out of bed, his silhouette framed against the moonlit window. "In the morning, I'm taking it to the pound where it belongs. And you can explain that to the girls."

In another moment, he was gone. She lay very still, staring into the darkness, waiting. But he didn't come back.

The bed beside her was still empty when she woke in the morning. Somewhere in the house, she could hear someone crying. Jumping up quickly, she pulled on jeans and a shirt and pulled a brush through her hair, then ran downstairs. The girls were out in back, sobbing as though their hearts would break.

"You told him," Cami cried accusingly as soon as she saw Kendall. "How could you tell him?"

"What?" Kendall looked from one to the other. "What's going on?"

"Daddy," Cami explained between sobs. "He's gone out to get Ricky Ticky."

They both wailed aloud. Kendall went down on her knees between them and pulled them both tightly to her, trying to quiet Tori, who was almost hysterical. "Hush now, your daddy's not going to hurt Ricky Ticky. We'll have to talk to him and see if we can convince him to change his mind."

"He-he-he'll kill him," Cami wailed. "He hates c-c-cats. One time, he said all cats should be drowned."

"Oh, honey, he was joking. He didn't really mean it."

Kendall looked up and saw Rafe on his way back to the house. Sure enough, he was carrying the basket. Feelings were running high, and she was getting almost as upset as the children. She rose to meet him, the girls clinging to her hands. His face was set sternly, and her heart skipped a beat.

"P-p-please, Daddy," Cami called out. "Please..."

Suddenly, Tori broke away and ran toward Rafe, her face wet with tears, contorted with emotion. When she reached him, her little fists began to pummel his legs.

"Hey," he said, looking down, holding the basket out of her reach.

Sobbing aloud, she beat as hard as she could. "Don't kill him, Daddy," she screamed out. "Don't kill him."

Rafe met Kendall's gaze in astonishment. "Tori, you spoke," he said, putting down the basket and going down on one knee to take her in his arms and hold her against him, stroking and patting to still her little arms and soothe her sobs. He kissed her hair, her face, and slowly, she began to calm.

"Tori, baby, please don't cry," he said as she began to control the sobs that racked her little body. "I need your help. Listen..." He pulled back and looked at her red face. "You have to tell me something. What's the kitten's name?"

"R-R-Ricky Ticky," she muttered, lower lip trembling.

"Good girl." He glanced at Kendall and winked. "Now tell me what you want to do with Ricky Ticky."

"I want to k-k-keep him."

Rafe nodded, and Kendall began to smile. It was obvious he was trying to keep her talking long enough to make it easier to stay verbal than to sink back into the silence again. When Cami strained to try to join them, Kendall held her back. The last thing Tori needed right now was someone trying to say her words for her.

"Where do you want to keep him?"

"In my room."

"In your room? Do you think that's a good place for a kitten?"

She nodded.

"Tell me in words, Tori."

"Yes," she said loud and clear. "Yes, I do."

"Tori, baby." He hugged her tight, his eyes closed. "You can have Ricky Ticky in your room. He's a darling little guy, and I think you deserve him."

She drew back, astonished, staring at him. "All for me?"

He nodded. "All for you." Then he glanced at where Cami stood, not knowing whether to feel happy or feel cheated. "And we'll just have to get another kitten for Cami to keep in her room. Okay?"

Cami let out a shriek of joy and raced to join in the hug. "Two kittens?" she asked Rafe, as though she could hardly believe it.

"Why not?" he said, grinning at her. "I've got two daughters. They ought to have two kittens."

Cami beamed, then looked a little sly. "But I'd really rather have Ricky Ticky," she tried, watching Rafe's reaction.

"Too bad, squirt," he said, tickling her. "This time Tori gets first choice."

Tori was glowing, and she didn't want to let go of her father, so Rafe hiked her up and held her in one arm for the next hour while they had breakfast and then prepared a place in her room for the cat. Kendall watched it all in wonder. It was going to be okay. Rafe had this marvelous capacity to grow and change, and that was something rare, something to be treasured. It was no wonder she loved him.

When Tori was settled with her new roommate, Rafe finally turned to Kendall. Silently, he led her into the bedroom and closed the door.

"Sorry about last night," he said. "I needed some time to think. I've got something I have to tell you."

"What, more?" she said ruefully. "I don't think I can take any more."

"This is serious. I've been lying to you. Here I am, blaming others for holding out on me, and I've been holding back the truth from you since the day we met."

Kendall folded her arms closely together, feeling suddenly cold. Sitting down on the bed, she tried to harden herself. Instinct told her it was going to be necessary. "What is it?" she asked, though she was sure she didn't really want to know.

He stared at her, his blue eyes piercing and opaque. "Darren left you at the altar because I told him to."

This was something so far off the wall, it took a moment for her to digest what he'd said. "What?"

"It was my fault. He was prepared to go through with it." Rafe turned and began to pace. "His friends threw a bachelor party for him, and he invited me over. I was sort of surprised. We hadn't spoken in a couple of years. But it was there that his friend Sam told me that you were a hussy using pregnancy to trap him into marriage. Knowing the sort of woman Darren usually went around with, I didn't question it at all. And he was obviously getting very shaky about the whole thing. He'd never been the marrying type, and he was beginning to wonder what the hell he was getting into."

Rafe paused and sat down beside Kendall. "So I told him to forget it. There were other ways to deal with this. I told him I would go and talk to... to you, explain he wasn't to be cornered that way. He thanked me for getting him off the hook. And I went to the church to give you the news."

Kendall felt as though she were moving in a dream. Reality had just crumbled around her. "Rafe, I can't believe this."

"I know. It was awful, cold, cruel, selfish. If I'd known you, I never would have done it."

But that wasn't good enough. Every assumption she had based their relationship on had just been swept away. Who was this man, really? Did she have any idea?

She stared at him, appalled. "How could you do that without knowing for sure? I could have really been pregnant. And all alone. And even if I had been some kind of bimbo, you know damn well that would have been as much Darren's responsibility as mine. How could you ignore that and act so coldly?"

"I don't know. I'm sorry." He shook his head, clearly anguished. "But in a way, I'm not sorry, because if I hadn't done it, you would probably be married to Darren right now."

That wasn't the point. "I can't believe you took my fate and turned it around without letting me know what was going on. You left me totally powerless, without any rights at all."

"Of course, I realize that now. Believe me, my views on this sort of thing have changed a lot. I used to be very cynical about women. I'm very ashamed of what I did. But I did do it. And I wanted you to know."

She turned blindly, heading for the stairs.

He watched her go, wanting to go after her, knowing that would be the worst thing to do right now. "Where are you going?"

She stopped, but she didn't look back. "I'm leaving. I have to go."

He swallowed hard. "I'll...I'll call you tomorrow."

"No, Rafe. Don't call me. I need time to think." She glanced back and wished she hadn't. "If you could do something like this to me—I don't know if I can forgive it." She stared at him, her eyes full of misery. "This is worse than what Darren did, you know. I mean, I can almost forgive him because I never expected that much of him in the first place. But you..." She shook her head. "I don't know, Rafe. I don't understand how you could have done that and not told me right away. I just don't know.''

She left, striding toward the stairway. Rafe stood very still, his arms hanging at his side. This couldn't be it. She'd come around by morning. There was no way he was prepared to lose her. Somehow, someway, he would get her back. In the meantime, he had a kitten to purchase.

"Kim, listen, I think I'm going to put new wallpaper up in the entryway. And while I'm at it, I think I'll get some new signs painted. And redo the landscaping out in front.''

Kim expired over her bookkeeping, facedown on the accounts-receivable column. "Good Lord, girl, when you say you're back, you really mean it. After two months of coming here on the fly, you're acting like a county health inspector. Every little detail is getting total scrutiny.''

"Well, it's about time, don't you think?'' Kendall frowned at the pictures of puppies hanging in the lobby. "These have got to go. I'm not into puppies any longer.''

"What shall we put up instead? Kittens?''

Kendall shook her head slowly. "No, not kittens.'' Babies. Wouldn't that be lovely? Fat, round babies, their little mouths so new and precious, their chubby little fingers reaching for butterflies... "No!'' she said vehemently.

Kim jumped. "Okay, okay. Forget I brought it up. I guess you're not much of an animal lover, are you?''

"Landscapes,'' Kendall said decisively. "Clouds and trees and sea scenes.''

"Nice. Without any people in them, I suppose?''

She turned and looked at her friend and fellow worker. "Why do you suppose that?"

"Because you seem to hate all of humanity since you broke up with Rafe," she said calmly. "What a grizzly bear. The kids are starting to leave your lessons with tears in their eyes."

"Oh, they are not."

"Well, they should be. You yell enough."

"I never yell."

"Tell that to the swim team. They were asking me to ship in a supply of earplugs."

"That was to keep water out of their ears."

Kim sniffed and looked superior. "Right."

Kendall glared at her and went into the pool area to check the filter and test the pH and chlorine levels of the water. She couldn't listen to any more of Kim's comments on her state of mind because she knew it was horrible. She missed Rafe so much, she could hardly stand it.

It had started out simply enough. She had needed time to get used to the fact that he had stopped her wedding. It had been a bitter pill to swallow, but she thought she would be able to get it out of her system and find a way to reconcile with him. Yet, the few times they had met, his attitude had only made things worse. He was arrogant about it, defensive. He wanted her to admit she was better off without Darren, so what he had done was all for the best. And she wouldn't do that. Why should she? He had done a terrible thing, and though he'd said he was sorry, she didn't believe him. She would have liked to see a little more humility.

It wouldn't kill her to go back to being alone, to coaching and teaching. She'd been doing fine before

Rafe had come into her life. She could go back to that. In fact, she could use the time to put together a more ambitious agenda for herself. She'd been drifting for too long. It was time to expand the swim school, take on a few more employees, get something moving. What was she, a woman or a wimp? She could do it.

But for just a moment, she indulged in a memory of Rafe, of his sweet smile, his hard, strong arms, his sensual kiss...and she was gasping for air, feeling like an addict going through withdrawal.

Rafe was pacing again, back and forth and up and down. It was monotonous, but necessary.

"Mr. Tennyson, you're going to wear a hole right through the floor," Grace told him, but he kept walking. He had to walk. What else could he do? Kendall had left him and it looked as though she wasn't coming back.

Grace spoke again. "Mr. Tennyson, I've got some things here you need to sign."

He stopped and stared at her. "Grace, why do you call me Mr. Tennyson when I call you Grace?"

She looked at him as though she weren't quite sure he was sane today. "Because that's your name, Mr. Tennyson. And my name's Grace. That's just the way it is."

"No, you know what I mean. If I can call you by your first name, you should be able to call me by my first name. Don't you think...?"

"Mr. Tennyson, I don't think. Administrative assistants are paid to think. I get a secretary's salary myself."

"Grace, I want you to call me Rafe from now on."

She looked a little nervous. "But what if I don't want to?"

He frowned. "I'm trying to be modern and equalitarian here. Not to mention losing my sexist state of mind."

"Mr. Tennyson, I don't need any handouts. I like calling you Mr. Tennyson. It makes you seem more important somehow. And I like to work for an important man." She measured him for a moment. "But if you really want to do something to improve my lot in life, I'll tell you what you can do. You can give me a shot at the position of administrative assistant. I think I could handle it nicely."

He grinned at her. She really was a prize. "You've got it, Grace. I'll put in a call to personnel." His expression hardened. "You do realize I'm going to hand over some of my responsibilities to you. I'm going to expect extra hours, extra creativity."

"I understand, sir. And I welcome it."

"Good. Now make me some coffee."

She grinned and paid no attention to him at all. It had been a long time, indeed, since she'd brewed a pot just for him.

"One more thing, sir," she said just before she left his office. "We're going to need a secretary, the two of us. Would you like me to give that information to personnel, as well?"

He laughed, his shoulders shaking. "I like your style, Grace. You do what you think is best. If I don't like it, I can always fire you."

"That you can, sir." She grinned and started to leave the office, then had second thoughts. Turning, she came back in, closing the door behind her. "Now that I'm your administrative assistant, Mr. Tennyson, I think I can also give you some advice."

He groaned. "Don't tell me I've created a monster," he growled.

"Here it is," she said, ignoring his comments. "Now, everybody in this place is scared of you. They don't know you like I do. I can see that big old cuddly bear beneath those sharp teeth, and I know your bark is worse than your bite. I also know all about Kendall McCormick and your relationship with her...."

"What?" His face turned red.

"And I know you and she have had a falling out. I just wanted to tell you, sir, that there's an old saying, 'faint heart never won fair lady.'" She shook a finger at him. "You better go after her before somebody else does, if you get my drift."

"I don't listen to drifts, Grace. You can take your advice and you can—"

"Eh, eh, eh." She held up her finger warningly. "Watch it. We wouldn't want to do anything that would look bad to our new administrative assistant, now would we?" She grinned. "I'll just run along to personnel."

She was gone in a flash, and Rafe was left to stare after her broodingly. He had a premonition that he was going to be spending a lot of time reminiscing about the good old days when Grace was a nice, quiet secretary.

But he knew her advice was right on the money. He could go after Kendall, or he could face life alone with his growing unhappiness. More than anything in the world, he needed Kendall back.

* * *

It had been two weeks since they had last seen each other, and Rafe couldn't take it anymore. He was beginning to remind himself of the polar bear he used to watch in the zoo, pacing back and forth all day. Grace was ordering new carpets, and he was about to book himself into a sanitarium. It was time to quit acting like a wimp. He had to get Kendall back. There was no other way to survive.

It was late in the evening when he went after her. He gave himself a motivational talking to, then drove up to the swim school, feeling like the Terminator. Watch out Kendall. I'm back.

Kim was just covering her computer as he entered the office. "Oh, hi, Rafe. Kendall is closing down the pool for the night, if you want to go on in. I've just got to lock up...."

Reaching out, he took the keys from her hand. "I'll do that for you. Why don't you go on home?"

"Oh." Kim stared at him, a bit overwhelmed. "Oh. Okay." She shuffled quickly toward the door, looking back. "You're sure?"

"I'm sure. Good night."

"Good night." She went out the door, and he locked it behind her.

Walking swiftly, he closed things down as he went, until he reached the pool area. He saw Kendall on the other side of the pool, putting away lane lines. Quietly, he locked the door from the inside, then started toward her.

He hadn't made a sound, but some sense must have told her she wasn't alone any longer. She straightened, her eyes widening, and she watched him come. He was ripping off his tie as he walked, throwing it aside. Then his fingers went for the buttons on his shirt.

"Oh, good," she said nervously as he approached. "We really do need to talk...."

"I didn't come to talk," he said calmly, dropping the shirt to the deck of the pool and reaching for his belt. He whipped it out and dropped it, taking the clipboard from her hand and throwing it aside, as well. "I came to show you something."

She was wearing the black swimsuit. He'd fantasized about that suit back in the days when he'd been consigned to merely watching swim lessons and not touching. He'd dreamed of ripping it from her body, among other things. But he wasn't going to do any ripping here. Just a little tugging.

With two quick movements, he hooked his hands under the fabric of her suit and pulled the top down, revealing breasts that always took his breath away. Her body was cool from her recent swim, the nipples high and dark, tight and huge. His own body stirred with desire as it always did when he saw her.

She reached up to stop him. "Rafe, don't! You can't. Kim..."

"Kim is gone. I watched her drive off. And I've locked every door in the place."

Her eyes were wide and tremulous, like a deer's. "But, we can't..."

"Can't we? You stand there trembling, with lips as red as cherries and nipples like knobs on a dresser, making me feel like I'm going to explode, and you tell me we can't?"

"But Rafe—"

Her lips were moist and full, and he tasted her excitement. She was as full of promise as ever, and he let her feel his growing need, a need that was as hard and sore as he had been that first time, crazy to have her.

Her protests were gone. She was as swept away as he was, her body on fire for his touch. Her hands sizzled on his bare skin, fingers raking across him as though she could gather him in and hold him close.

"Hold me. Oh, Rafe, I need you...."

He slipped the swimsuit down until it fell away, and she arched back, rubbing her breasts against him, crying out when his mouth closed on her nipple.

"Oh, Rafe, I need you now...."

"Not yet," he murmured, kissing her skin, her ear, her hair. "Not yet, my love. I need to take in all of you, every part I've missed so much."

She ground her hips against his, the raw, animal need coming up in a growl from her throat. And then she was on the floor, her back against the cold cement of the pool deck, but she didn't care. She held him with her legs, urging him in, moving her hips in a dance of enticement that came from primeval instinct rather than design.

"Now, Rafe, now!"

"Not yet, I—"

With a growl that seemed to fill the room, she lifted her hips and brought him inside, capturing him, holding him, making him thrust harder and harder, because she seemed to need him so much more. Her cries came faster and faster, and his gasping breath filled her head just as he filled her body.

"I love you, Kendall," he seemed to be saying.

But that couldn't be right. He'd never said that before, and anyway, there was no time to stop and analyze. She was reaching for paradise, running harder and harder, flying higher and higher, stretching to savor every drop.

"Oh," she gasped at last, falling back down into reality. "If it ever gets any better than that, I'll die."

"It will get better," he promised. "And you won't die. But you will go to heaven."

She rose on her elbow to look at him, still breathing hard. "You jerk," she said, grinning. "You didn't even let me make you crawl first."

He smiled and reached to touch her face. "I had no intention of crawling. But I will get down on one knee."

"Hmm? What for?"

"This."

True to his word, he rose painfully and tried to get into position.

She frowned, watching him. "What are you doing?"

"I'm trying to get set to ask you to marry me."

She went still as death, scared to ask for a repeat.

He looked at her. "Did you hear what I said?"

She shook her head slowly, staring at him. "No. Say it again."

He took her hands in his and tried to smile, but he was too anxious about her answer. "Will you marry me, Kendall?"

So she really had heard those words. She still couldn't believe it. "But, Rafe," she said dreamily, "this is so sudden."

"Sudden? We've been sleeping together for six weeks."

"Yes, but..." She shook her head, still bewildered by the speed of his conversion. "You never said anything about getting married."

"No, I guess I never did." Drawing her hands to his lips, he kissed them softly and repeatedly. "I thought I'd wait until I wanted to before I mentioned it. Was I wrong?"

"No, I suppose not." She was floating in a dream. This couldn't be real, could it? "But I don't know what to say."

He took her head, fingers threading through her thick hair, and pulled her to him, kissing her lips. "Say yes, darling," he whispered, love in his eyes. "It's the accepted thing."

"Yes." She clung to him. "Oh, yes, Rafe. I love you so much."

Twelve

The preparations for the wedding were moving along swiftly. Rafe was in a hurry. He wanted to make sure he and Kendall were married before Darren got back. He still couldn't make himself believe that she might love him and not Darren. But he didn't let himself care anymore. He wanted her anyway, even after all he'd gone through with Marci. He was ready to risk it. He loved Kendall so much, the thought of losing her was unacceptable. He couldn't even look the possibility square in the face. He wouldn't lose her. He couldn't lose her. No matter what. He had to marry her and make her deliriously happy before Darren returned and ruined everything.

And so he hung around while decisions were being made, trying to talk her into eloping immediately, and when that didn't work, trying to move up the time of the wedding to something like next week.

Kendall was going nuts. There was so much to plan, so much to do. Where should they have the wedding? When should they have it? Who should be invited?

"Let's invite everybody we know," Rafe said grandly, once the idea of eloping had been shot down. "I want everyone in town to witness it."

"A few chosen friends," Kendall countered. "A small chapel in the woods."

In the end, they settled for having the wedding at his house—"That way you won't be able to run away at least," Kendall had commented—with an invitation list that included only half the known universe.

"Are you going to want a bachelor party?" she asked Rafe, remembering what had happened at Darren's.

"Are you kidding? I've been a bachelor for too long as it is. I'm certainly not going to celebrate it. I just want to get married."

The perfect answer. But why not? She was marrying the perfect man.

Rafe's best friend since forever, Robert Kraemer, was flying in from out of town to be best man. Kim had agreed to be Kendall's maid of honor—again.

"As long as you don't think that would jinx things," she said worriedly.

"If anyone's the jinx, it's got to be me," Kendall reassured her. "And I wouldn't want anyone else but you, anyway."

She told Kim not to try to give her a shower. "I just had a shower a few months ago. I certainly don't deserve another one."

But Mrs. McReady thought otherwise and surprised Kendall with one just the same. When Kendall arrived at the restaurant for lunch, she found it filled with balloons and presents and friends from everywhere. It was such a touching moment, and her eyes pooled with tears.

"Don't get sloppy, dear," Mrs. McReady advised. "We'll eat and thank all the nice people for bringing you these presents and send them on their way. Then I'll stay to help you open the gifts. That's my favorite part."

Cami and Tori were ecstatic. They spent hours being fitted in little gowns that were miniatures of what Kendall was wearing, one in pink and one in yellow. "Cuz in a way, we're all getting married to each other, huh?" Cami commented to general laughter and agreement.

The wedding gown was simple and elegant, embroidered with satin piping and edged with pearl beading. The sleeves were elbow length, the bodice fitted, the neckline flat and oval. The veil was anchored by satin rosebuds. It was a gown to take your breath away—and as different from the one she had worn to marry Darren as she could possibly get it to be.

"No man who sees you in this would ever jilt you," her mother said in her blunt, humorous way.

Kendall had to agree. She looked darn beautiful.

Rafe was a nervous wreck by the time the wedding day dawned. He supervised building the gazebo and setting up the fountain and arranging the tables for the food, the rented chairs for the guests. And when it was time for him to go and get himself shaved and showered and shoved into his tuxedo, he went into a white panic.

It was almost time. She was almost his. Just two more hours. Then an hour and a half. An hour. People were beginning to arrive. He was dressed and ready, and he knew Kendall was upstairs getting into her gown, but he couldn't stay put. He had to roam among the guests, greeting old friends when he could calm down enough to recognize them.

He had just completely ignored his old Business Law professor from college when the maid waylaid him. "Mr. Tennyson, I've been looking all over for you. There's a gentleman waiting to speak to you in the library. He said it was urgent."

"In the library?" Let's see, where was that again?

"Yes, sir."

"Oh, all right." Down the hall, turn left. At least, that was where it used to be. "Thank you, Betty."

Rafe walked down the hall, his mind in a haze, and opened the door to come face-to-face with his long-lost brother.

Rafe crashed back to earth with a thump that left his ears ringing. "Darren," he said coolly. "I see you made it back."

His blond, handsome brother stared right back. "And just in time, Rafe. Just in time."

Rafe nodded, his adrenaline racing. "You came for the wedding?" Where was Kendall? Had she seen Darren yet?

Darren didn't answer Rafe's question directly. He sneered, his eyes blazing, and said, "Just let me get one thing straight, brother dear. Did you really talk me out of marrying her so you could have her for yourself?"

Rafe knew his brother had a case, but he wasn't about to give him any ground. "Darren, I didn't even know her at that point. I thought..."

"What did you think? I don't understand. I mean, I look back, I regret it—leaving Kendall, walking out on her, listening to you. I come back to see if I can make things right, and what do I find? My brother's marrying her."

"Face it, Darren. You didn't want to marry her. You didn't want to marry anyone. You begged me to get you off the hook."

"That wasn't how it was, and you know it. You talked me into it. How do you think she's going to feel when I tell her it was all your idea?"

Rafe frowned. Not only was Darren a jerk, he was self-delusional. "You never loved her. If you had, you wouldn't have let anything stop your wedding."

Darren grimaced and looked away, anger steeped in years of bitterness flashing from him. "Damn you, Rafe, you want everything for yourself." Whirling, he shook a fist at his brother, anger making his voice tremble. "Well you're not going to get her. I can get her back with a snap of my fingers. She was dying for me, man. And when I go up and show her I'm back, she's going to fall all over me."

He headed for the door, and Rafe didn't do anything to stop him. He stood where he was for a moment, then followed his brother out into the living room and watched him climb the stairs.

People spoke to him, but Rafe didn't hear a word. He was fixated on Darren's progress, and his heart was in his throat.

Darren spoke to someone on his way up, smiled and laughed at a joke, then turned and rapped his knuckles against the door to the room where Kendall was getting ready for the ceremony. The door opened. He said something. He was smiling. A hand reached out, a slender arm. Kendall's arm. Darren was pulled inside the room and the door was closed. Rafe felt as though a bullet had just gone through his heart.

He couldn't just stand here waiting to see what would happen. Turning, he headed for the kitchen, away from the crowd that was gathering. He walked through without acknowledging any of the staff and went on out the back door, heading for the garage where he kept his antique M.G. In a few moments, he was roaring down the driveway.

Kendall's mother had witnessed his escape from where she was sitting with Kendall's father on the deck, sipping long, cool drinks. She turned to her husband and nudged him. "The groom has just left the building. What do you suppose this means?"

He shrugged and went on contemplating his iced tea. "I don't know, Marge, but I'd say it just might be déjà vu all over again." He shook his head and took a long sip. "They don't do these things the way they used to. Have you noticed that?"

This time, though, the groom came back. He walked in just as the organist began to play her prelude.

"Where have you been?" Robert demanded, grabbing him. "It's time to start. We've got to walk down the aisle and take our places."

Rafe nodded absently. He didn't see Darren anywhere. Did that mean he was still in the room with Kendall? Or did it mean the two of them had taken off together?

Never mind. He would walk down the aisle and stand there like a fool, waiting for nobody.

The music swelled. Robert gripped Rafe's arm and shoved him toward where the minister, Dr. Petersen, was waiting. Rafe put one foot ahead of the other, moving like a robot toward the altar with its carnations and chrysanthemums.

Then Rafe and Robert stood ready. Dr. Petersen stood in his vestments, bible in his hand. The organist started up "Here Comes the Bride." But no one started down the aisle. Guests were turning their heads, straining to see a bride who wasn't there. Anger fought with anguish in Rafe's chest. Was he just going to stay here and take this, or was he going to go after them?

Damn it, Darren was no good for her. Didn't she know that? He turned, ready to get back in his car and race out after Darren and force him to give her up.

But suddenly, there she was, coming down the aisle toward him, and his heart leaped into his throat. He blinked, not sure if he could believe his own eyes. But it was she. And she was the most beautiful thing he had ever seen.

Kendall came up beside him, smiling through her veil. "Sorry," she whispered. "My train got caught."

"Where's Darren?" he whispered back, under cover of the still-thundering organ solo.

"Gone." She smiled at him. "He told me about your encounter. About his threat to take me away." She laughed, shaking her head. "Can you believe that guy? What an ego."

Rafe reached out and took her in his arms, heedless of the shocked murmuring of the audience. "I was so afraid..." He couldn't finish the sentence.

Pulling back, Kendall looked into his eyes with wonder. "Rafe, you can't possibly still be afraid I would pick him over you. Don't you understand? Darren is a boy. I don't know if he'll ever grow up."

She touched his face with her fingertips. "You're a man, darling. And real women marry real men. Believe me, things work out best that way."

He pushed aside her veil and kissed her, his heart so full he had to show it somehow.

"Hey, wait a minute," the minister said. "That's not in the script. You've got to wait until she says 'I do.'"

Rafe grinned at the minister, at the world at large. "She just said it, Dr. Petersen. Loud and clear."

The minister shrugged good-naturedly. "Well, then, kiss away you two. We'll go on with the ceremony when you're ready."

And to the scattered applause and laughter from the congregation, they did.

* * * * *

HARLEQUIN®

Don't miss these Harlequin favorites by some of our most distinguished authors!
And now, you can receive a discount by ordering two or more titles!

HT #25663	THE LAWMAN by Vicki Lewis Thompson	$3.25 U.S.☐/$3.75 CAN. ☐
HP #11788	THE SISTER SWAP by Susan Napier	$3.25 U.S.☐/$3.75 CAN. ☐
HR #03293	THE MAN WHO CAME FOR CHRISTMAS by Bethany Campbell	$2.99 U.S.☐/$3.50 CAN. ☐
HS #70667	FATHERS & OTHER STRANGERS by Evelyn Crowe	$3.75 U.S.☐/$4.25 CAN. ☐
HI #22198	MURDER BY THE BOOK by Margaret St. George	$2.89 ☐
HAR #16520	THE ADVENTURESS by M.J. Rodgers	$3.50 U.S.☐/$3.99 CAN. ☐
HH #28885	DESERT ROGUE by Erin Yorke	$4.50 U.S.☐/$4.99 CAN. ☐

(limited quantities available on certain titles)

	AMOUNT	$
DEDUCT:	**10% DISCOUNT FOR 2+ BOOKS**	$
ADD:	**POSTAGE & HANDLING**	$
	($1.00 for one book, 50¢ for each additional)	
	APPLICABLE TAXES**	$_____
	TOTAL PAYABLE	$_____
	(check or money order—please do not send cash)	

To order, complete this form and send it, along with a check or money order for the total above, payable to Harlequin Books, to: **In the U.S.:** 3010 Walden Avenue, P.O. Box 9047, Buffalo, NY 14269-9047; **In Canada:** P.O. Box 613, Fort Erie, Ontario, L2A 5X3.

Name: _____

Address: _____ City: _____

State/Prov.: _____ Zip/Postal Code: _____

**New York residents remit applicable sales taxes.
Canadian residents remit applicable GST and provincial taxes.   HBACK-JS3

Look us up on-line at: http://www.romance.net

Harlequin Romance ®

Delightful

Affectionate

Romantic

Emotional

Tender

Original

Daring

Riveting

Enchanting

Adventurous

Moving

**Harlequin Romance—the
series that has it all!**

HROM-G

HARLEQUIN PRESENTS®

HARLEQUIN PRESENTS
men you won't be able to resist falling in love with...

HARLEQUIN PRESENTS
women who have feelings just like your own...

HARLEQUIN PRESENTS
powerful passion in exotic international settings...

HARLEQUIN PRESENTS
intense, dramatic stories that will keep you turning
to the very last page...

HARLEQUIN PRESENTS
The world's bestselling romance series!

Harlequin® Historical

If you're a serious fan of historical romance,
then you're in luck!

Harlequin Historicals brings you
stories by bestselling authors, rising new stars
and talented first-timers.

Ruth Langan & Theresa Michaels
Mary McBride & Cheryl St. John
Margaret Moore & Merline Lovelace
Julie Tetel & Nina Beaumont
Susan Amarillas & Ana Seymour
Deborah Simmons & Linda Castle
Cassandra Austin & Emily French
Miranda Jarrett & Suzanne Barclay
DeLoras Scott & Laurie Grant...

You'll never run out of favorites.

Harlequin Historicals...they're too good to miss!

Jane Fonda
and
Roger Vadim

In 1964, when French film director, Roger Vadim, asked Jane Fonda to do a picture for him, she flatly declined, calling him "perverse, despicable and hateful." But he won her over. She not only did the film *La Ronde* with him, she also moved in with him. Later, he directed her in the 1968 cult classic, *Barbarella*.

The couple bought a home in Malibu and lived together for a year before deciding to marry in 1965.

With twenty-plus friends and family in tow, they boarded a chartered plane and headed to The Dunes hotel in Las Vegas for the ceremony. The same justice of the peace who married Cary Grant and Dyan Cannon presided. Interestingly, though, Jane neglected to sign the marriage application.

The marriage ended in divorce in 1969—the split due largely to Roger's admitted liaisons.

B-FONDA